P9-DJK-407

NEW TECUMSETH
Property of
PUBLIC LIBRARY
DISCARD

LOCKWOOD

LOCKWOOD

Lauran Paine

Thorndike Press • Chivers Press
Thorndike, Maine USA Bath, England

This Large Print edition is published by Thorndike Press, USA and by Chivers Press, England.

Published in 1997 in the U.S. by arrangement with Golden West Literary Agency.

Published in 1997 in the U.K. by arrangement with Golden West Literary Agency.

U.S. Hardcover 0-7862-1121-0 (Western Series Edition)
U.K. Hardcover 0-7540-3082-2 (Chivers Large Print)

Thorndike Large Print® Western Series.

The text of this Large Print edition is unabridged.
Other aspects of the book may vary from the original edition.

Set in 16 pt. Plantin by Al Chase.

Printed in the United States on permanent paper.

British Library Cataloguing in Publication Data available

Library of Congress Cataloging in Publication Data

Paine, Lauran.
Lockwood : a western story / by Lauran Paine.
p. cm.
ISBN 0-7862-1121-0 (lg. print : hc : alk. paper)
1. Large type books. I. Title.
PS3566.A34L58 1997
813′.54—dc21 97-18661

LOCKWOOD

Chapter One

SPRINGTIME

Winter died with a long, wet sigh. Spring arrived with a warm wind; the red buds blossomed; shy alfilaria provided a ground-hugging carpet with its tiny lavender flowers. Cottonwoods showed pale green leaves along with the fingerlings that within a couple of months would shed their cotton. Birds quarreled, carried twigs, and sang. Trout minnows darted and swarmed, sweeping first one way then another.

Nature recreated her world, so it was said and believed, for the benefit of man whose cattle lost their winter dullness, shed off shiny, tucked new tallow under multicolored hides, went off to secret places to calve, and coyotes fattened on what was left — afterbirth.

Grass throve in warm, wet soil; weeds flourished along creeks; and willows budded. There was no other time of the year when sap ran so strongly, when creatures mated in the knowledge they would bear young when food was plentiful. The moon helped during its cyclical swelling toward ghostly fullness. Days were warm; nights cold. The in between times it was cool but no longer cold.

Winter shortened perspectives. Townsfolk no longer picnicked in the foothills. Stockmen remained close to their yards. People, like other animals, waited out winter close to heat and food. Springtime changed that: animals coursed; people traveled; life, like tree sap, ran.

There would be rain, but it would be warm; life required it. Animals with four legs or two legs welcomed rain, particularly in stock country. Even the solitary horseman enjoyed rain inside his black poncho which shone with water like black gold. The footing was soft, but he was in no hurry as he traveled around the knobs he could avoid and breasted the long-running ribs he could not avoid.

His direction was southeast. Not that it mattered much. He was crossing new country after two years' straight running in the vicinity of a town in northern Wyoming above the Laramie Plains called Bitterroot, a mining town in the middle of cattle country. He had stayed because he had to but had never liked mining communities or most of the folks who inhabited them. They were usually dirty; some were more unpleasant than others. They seemed to lack the openness of livestock people, and he had been raised with livestock, not miners. At thirty-one he hadn't been able to make a thorough adjustment, so he had quit, saddled up, and headed out — at the best time for creatures to travel when nature provided what travelers required.

He had been on the trail for some time. He did not own a watch nor would one have helped. He did not know which month it was and that didn't matter much either. There were occasional great white cloud galleons sailing across azure skies and nights when every star winked hard brightness in its black setting, dark green grass, not pale green new grass that scoured livestock, but dark green that nourished them.

The land he was traversing was flat to rolling, almost treeless, with distant grazing cattle. Twice he startled bands of horses. Both times they put their tails in the air and raced over the horizon. They weren't inbred, wormy mustangs; they had been someone's loose stock, well bred, quality animals. Shortly now they would be rounded up, have the kinks worked out, and put to work. Springtime was also marking and branding time. When full summer arrived, they would cover miles under saddle watching for screw worms, hung-up calves, wolves that attacked, and skulking coyotes that waited in hiding to kill by stealth.

He rolled a brown-paper cigarette, lighted up, inhaled, exhaled, and told his horse the country they were passing over was good. The horse, accustomed to being talked to, paid no attention. He had seen movement far ahead, partially obscured by flourishing creek willows where a watercourse ran in a meandering way. The man saw nothing; the movement was hidden from sight along the creek where willows grew as thick as the hair on a dog's back.

The sun was directly overhead. A man's shadow for this brief period of each day was beneath his feet. Ground-nesting birds exploded from their secret places as shod-horse reverberations caused panic. Even a small, neckless ground owl was routed out of his hole. The man watched him flying blind, or nearly blind, in a way indicating the owl had no destination, just escape.

He stopped once where a cairn of stones showed in the grass. Another month and the grass would be too tall. Right now the grave was visible, and old. Probably very old because mounded rocks had tumbled from the top. There was no headboard, nothing at all to denote who was buried there except the rocks in the grave shape.

The man said, “In’ian?” As a blow fly buzzed the horse’s nostrils, it shook its head. The man agreed. “Naw. In’ians didn’t bury ’em out like this. They hid graves. Or they had secret places where they made mummy bundles an’ put ’em on platforms.”

The rider squeezed, and the horse moved out. The animal was well muscled and short backed. He didn’t carry an ounce of fat, and his hide was shiny. He was in his prime, neither young nor old, seven going onto eight.

His rider had steel-blue eyes, a hide browned from exposure. He sat a horse like it was an extended part of him. His saddle had the maker’s name on the seating leather up near the gullet, and where it had been made. Miles City, Montana.

The man was about average height, maybe a tad less. He was lean and muscular. Now he was wearing doeskin riding gloves, but ordinarily he kept them folded over and under his shell belt.

He had even features, neither coarse nor pinched. His mouth more than his eyes mirrored character. The lips were thin but not tight. To some, usually old women who could read a man’s face, he appeared as rather tolerant, probably easy-going, sensible but uncompromising. It was a fair assessment.

The land gradually rose toward a mile-distant drop-off which was not precipitate. Nothing in this country was precipitate. The land rolled and tapered off the same way. Within sixty days grass heads would brush a man's stirrups.

When he topped the rib of land, he halted again. Below and onward a fair distance was a willow creek, its water completely hidden by tangled growth on both sides. There were birds down there noisily staking out nest sites. There was also a doe with twin spotted fawns who had seen the man the instant he appeared against the horizon.

She watched, chewed, made no move to herd her babies until the man started down the slope in her direction. Even then she did not run but simply took high steps with her youngsters, who had seen nothing, and moved farther south along the creek. She never did run. She merely put distance between herself and the oncoming rider then faded from sight among the creek willows.

The sun had passed so that the rider's shadow was in front now as he reached the creek, sat a moment considering, then swung off, hobbled his horse first before removing the saddle, bridle, and blanket. The horse went through willows to drink. It paused after tanking up, peering northward. There was the faint scent of another horse. It backed out of the willows to crop grass. Hunger came first.

The man up-ended his saddle, draped the sweaty blanket on the willows wet-side up, freed his tight-wound blanket roll from behind the saddle, and flung it out. In strange country knowledgeable travelers did not end their day with sundown. They ended it where they found a place with water and grass.

He gathered dead wood for his supper fire, stood a while breathing the faint aroma of shy flowers, then shucked out of his clothes, went down to the creek where the water was as cold as a witch's bosom, scrubbed, found a place where sunlight reached, and sat there to dry off, something that would require less time in another month or two. He went back, dressed, spread flat out atop the bedroll, and made a smoke. He was drowsy as he lay there watching the busy birds, some carrying twigs into the willows, others fighting to protect their nesting sites, some sitting as high as they could get, scolding the two-legged trespasser.

Abruptly, for no perceptible reason, all the birds which had been so preoccupied moments before, took wing and, like wind-blown autumn leaves, flew in all directions. The man didn't move for a long moment, then he sat up, stubbed out his smoke, and slowly turned his head. His shell belt and holstered Colt were hanging ten feet away on a willow limb.

He didn't see her until she stepped forward, moving away from a background of willows. She was wearing a doehide split riding skirt and a light tan blouse. Her eyes were brown. Her hair, with shards of sunlight touching it, shone brown with a faint reddish tinge.

She said: "Hello."

He repeated it. "Hello."

It occurred to him that she had probably been standing back in there while he had bathed. His face colored as she came closer. Embarrassment rarely lingered. In this case he still had the feeling, but she minimized it as she plucked a grass stalk and chewed it, with her eyes laughing at him. She sat down in the grass, pulled up both legs, and hooked her arms around them.

"It's beautiful, isn't it?"

He nodded. She had meant the area. He had meant *she* was beautiful. It had been a long time — a very long time.

She turned her head. She really was laughing at him. He guessed her to be past girlhood by maybe five or six years. She had a straightforward manner he was not accustomed to. She said: "Who are you?"

"Lockwood. Who are you?"

"Shelly Harrison. My real name is Shelbourne. I was supposed to be a boy. Isn't that an awful name for a girl?"

He hung fire before replying. "I don't know. I once knew a woman named Jonny."

"Really? That's terrible."

He nodded slightly. "It's unusual, for a fact. She was named after her father. His name was Jonathan. They shortened it to Jonny."

Up close her eyes had the same faint hint of red-gold that her hair had. He had never seen a human being with eyes that shade before.

"Are you looking for work?" she asked.

He was getting more relaxed by the moment. "No. Not exactly. I was heading south . . . somewhere."

"Somewhere?"

"Up north they get snow hip pocket high to a tall In'ian. The winters are fierce. I'm going where the seasons are shorter in winter and longer in summer."

She laughed at him. "Do you know where that is?"

"No."

"Heaven," she said, and laughed again.

He smiled. "I'm not in a hurry to find out. I was thinking more like New Mexico."

"Have you ever been there?"

"No, ma'am. Have you?"

"Once, to visit an aunt who died a few years back. It's all right up north, but the farther south you go the drier and hotter and more desolate it is."

"I'll stay up north, then. Where's your horse?"

She jerked her head. "A half mile or so up yonder. . . . I like this place . . . it's private . . . mostly anyway . . . and peaceful. I've been coming up here every spring since I got rid of my pigtails."

"You live close by, ma'am?"

"Yes. About four miles southeast." She gestured. "Harrison ranch covers thirty miles in all directions. My grandfather came here after the war, worked himself almost to death, and died. I never knew him, but my mother says my father is exactly like him." She sighed and looped both arms around her knees again as she watched the creek sparkle in sunlight. After a moment she roused from her reverie and said: "My father's hiring on, Mister Lockwood."

He smiled at her. "It snows in Wyoming."

She laughed at him. "But not as much as

in Montana, Mister Lockwood."

"Three, four feet on the flat, ma'am?"

"Rarely. Mostly it gets maybe a foot deep, sometimes two feet."

"From September until March?"

"Oh no. More like December to February, with occasional flurries in March. Does that tempt you, Mister Lockwood?"

He felt heat in his cheeks as their eyes met and held when he said: "No ma'am, *that* don't."

She did not turn away immediately, but eventually she did, to sit with arms hooked, legs drawn up, solemnly considering the empty run of seemingly endless grassland.

He said: "Sun's slanting away."

She did not respond for a moment or two. "I'm not afraid of the dark."

"But your folks'll worry. Your maw will. . . ."

"She's visitin' her folks back East." The dark eyes came around to him.

He sought words, couldn't find the right ones, and wisely said nothing.

"Mister Lockwood . . . ?"

"Yes ma'am?"

"Do you have enough food for two?"

"Yes, ma'am."

"Would you mind if I stayed?"

This time he really had trouble finding

words. "Well, your paw'll. . . ."

"He's down in Denver."

"Oh. You folks got hired hands?"

"Yes, four full-time riders and a range boss called Temple. His real name is Templeton Burroughs."

"They'll worry, ma'am."

"Mister Lockwood . . . just Shelly. Is that all right?"

It most certainly was. He nodded.

"They won't worry. They'll head for town. With Paw gone, they do about as they please. To them I'm someone to be avoided whether Paw's home or not. What's your first name?"

"Cuff. That's not my name, but that's what I've been called since I was six or eight years old."

"What is your real name?"

"Saul. I never liked it either."

"It's a nice name, but I like Cuff better."

"My folks was religious. It's a name out of the Bible."

She nodded as she arose. "Where's the coffee pot? Do you have a fry pan? I'll scrub the pan at the creek and fill the pot."

He dug them out of his gatherings along with two tin plates and two forks. He watched her go to the creek and bend down. He made a little dry-wood fire with creek-willows for a background, went across the creek to see how his horse was doing and, when he returned, she was busy at the fire.

He asked her about her horse and she shrugged. “The bridle’s hanging on the horn, and he’s hobbled.”

Dusk arrived to be followed by a black sky until a belated moon appeared. There were coyotes sounding northward when she said, “What is that on your left shoulder, Cuff?”

“A birthmark.”

“It’s shaped almost like a horseshoe.”

Chapter Two

TROUBLE IN A NEW COUNTRY

Springtime had its vagaries like any other time of the year. It was overcast when he left, the sky gray from horizon to horizon, which did not help any. Twice he twisted to look back. She was standing where their little cooking fire had died. He waved. The first time she waved back. The second time she didn't.

He crossed a stage road where a town lay distantly visible. What remained of a shotgun-targeted sign with an arrow pointing southward said **Dunston.** One blast had obliterated the number which came next and had almost obliterated the word **miles.** He guessed Dunstan was about three miles south. He did not turn down the road. He had supplies, but the main reason he did not go down there was that he was reliving a vivid and breath-taking memory. He wanted to be alone with it.

For two days he rode steadily southeast, stopping at only one town when he ran out of grub. After filling his saddle bags, he continued southeasterly. The town had a saloon; in fact it had several. It also had a cafe, something he would have enjoyed after months of eating out of the same tin plate, drinking the same bad coffee, but his private mood lingered. He did not want to be around people.

Two weeks later he rode into a pleasant place called Derby. It had shade trees, stores, public troughs, three cafes, and one particularly noticeable saloon whose front had been painted rusty red with the spindle-doors dark brown. He put up at the rooming house after making certain his horse would be adequately cared for by the thick-necked, burly livery man whose face showed two eyes, a nose, and a long, wide mouth while everything else was covered by hair.

Spring was sliding along toward summer. Folks were busy; most seemed friendly. His first night in a bed off the ground he heard someone playing a piano and singing "Lorena." In the morning he was awakened by the smith at the lower end of town shaping steel over an anvil.

The woman who owned the rooming house was Mrs. Bradley. She was almost as broad as she was tall. She was a widow woman with enough age on her not to be fooled nor surprised. They sat on the verandah one evening after supper and talked for an hour about her late husband, the town, the people, even the weather. She told Lockwood the livery man, whose name was Abel Starr, had been courting her off and on for several years.

She snorted as they sat gazing southward down through town. "Kissin' that man," she said bluntly, "would be like kissin' a bear's behind."

Lockwood inhaled, exhaled, recovered from shock, and was ready to go to his room when the sturdy woman said something else. "But Abel's a good man. When they tried to rob the store last year 'n' after they wounded the town marshal, Abel stood wide legged in the center of the barn doorway, shot it out with 'em, and killed them both." She shifted in the old chair and sighed. "If he'd shave his face . . . maybe. So far, an' I've known him six years, I don't even know what he looks like."

The following day at the pool hall the proprietor, a crippled older man who left his chair near the front door only when it could not be avoided, watched Lockwood and the farrier's helper shoot a game. Lockwood was good. He won four out of five games.

After the smith's helper departed, the old man patted a chair and said: "Set, mister."

Lockwood paid the proprietor twenty-five cents for the use of the table out of his winnings and sat down. The old man had shrewd eyes and a big bump of curiosity. He also had poor manners. Folks did not ask strangers personal questions, but the pool hall proprietor did and seemed not the least abashed. Being a cripple had advantages.

"I've seen you around town the last few days. You got a name?"

"Cuff Lockwood. You got one?"

"Billy Phelps. I busted a hip years back when a stage turned over. What d'you do for a living, Mister Lockwood?"

A pair of bewhiskered burly men in checkered plaid shirts passed as Lockwood answered. "Nothing right now. I worked stock in Montana and northern Wyoming until I dang near froze through the winters. Now, I'm goin' to go south until no one spikes their horseshoes to keep animals from fallin' on the ice."

Billy Phelps chased a fly off his bald dome, leaned, and spat amber into a box of sand across the doorway. "You married, Mister Lockwood?"

The reply was slow. "No. Why? You got a daughter?"

Billy Phelps snorted. "Couldn't get me a wife after the accident to make one with.

Did you see them two freighters who walked by a few minutes ago? Well, it was men like them killed our town marshal a month back. Since then they've done about as they pleased, even to drivin' big rigs with ten upright down the main street of town, despite that we got an ordnance for them to go around back an' not block traffic on Main Street."

Lockwood was listening. He was also watching a woman wearing a large black hat who was riding as pretty a chestnut with four white socks as he had ever seen. He said: "There's a horse worth seventy-five dollars."

The pool hall proprietor had to lean to see around the jamb of the roadway door. He grunted and settled back. "That's Lady Barlow. Widow woman. She owns a big ranch northeast of town." Billy Phelps turned to study Lockwood's profile. "An' she don't like men. Not one bit. Not even her range boss who's been with the outfit since before her husband died. She's tougher'n rawhide, meaner'n a cougar, and owns the local bank. Forget about talkin' her out of that chestnut. It was the last present from her husband before he died."

Lockwood gazed at the old man as he asked how come the pool hall proprietor knew so much. Billy Phelps aimed for the sandbox before replying. "I set here 'n' sooner or later everything folks say comes to me through fellers who come in to shoot a few games. Mister Lockwood, you ever done lawman work?"

Lockwood gazed at the old man. Since entering the pool hall, he'd speculated about the pot-bellied, shrewd-eyed proprietor. After sitting and visiting with him, he had begun to suspect Billy's questions had a purpose. Now, he thought, he knew what it was.

He did not give a direct answer to the question. He said: "How much snow do you get in an average winter?"

Billy's brow dropped, his gaze showing bafflement. "What's that got to do with law enforcement, Mister Lockwood?"

"I told you, Mister Phelps, the next place I stop riding is goin' to be where I don't freeze my nose."

Billy leaned as far forward as he dared and jutted his jaw. "Across the road there you see them lighter boards from the ground up on the jailhouse wall? Well, that's how deep the snow gets. Not every winter but close enough." Billy settled back. "It's a nice tight jailhouse. The town furnishes wood for the stove. There's a shed out back an' a good corral. Wintertime in Derby is like a funeral. Mostly folks hole up. Stages come along when they can. Them troublesome freighters don't come at all. It's a good job, Mister Lockwood. Pays as much as a range boss makes an' you can set inside most of the time."

Lockwood gazed dispassionately across the road at that bleached-pale lower siding on the jailhouse. It was at least two feet from the ground. He shoved his legs out, clasped hands across his middle, and gently shook his head. "That's too much snow, Mister Phelps."

The older man snorted. "Two feet? We don't always get that much. You asked and I answered. But most winters we don't get more'n an occasional skiff."

Lockwood gazed at Billy Phelps. This was still Wyoming, and any part of Wyoming that only got light skiffs of snow did not exist. Lockwood leaned forward and shot up to his feet. "It's been nice talkin' to you, Mister Phelps," he said and walked outside where two-legged, four-legged, and wheeled traffic passed in both directions. For a fact Derby was a flourishing place.

He went down to the cafe on the same side of the road as the pool hall, next door to an abstract office and one more place, the local bank, a fine brick structure with steel shutters on both sides of the roadway windows painted black. He'd never heard of a female owning a bank.

The counter was fairly full. The cafe man shot Lockwood a harassed glance as he passed bearing dinner plates. There was smoke and talk, even an occasional jibe among men who knew each other, and laughter.

Lockwood sat down between two bewhiskered men, one large and massive, the other thin as a snake and no taller than average. They were both eating soup, filtering it through beards and sounding like critters pulling feet out of mud.

The sweating cafe man hesitated. "Fried spuds, antelope steak, pie, an' coffee?"

Lockwood nodded. The cafe man sped away with more platters, eventually brought Lockwood's coffee, barely hesitated as he did this, then went swiftly back to his cooking area. The skinny man spoke to Lockwood. "What he needs is a squaw in the kitchen an' him out front."

Lockwood nodded as the lean man shoved an empty bowl away and leaned around Lockwood to address the large, bearded man on Lockwood's right side.

"You finished yet?"

The bear-like man growled. "No. Shut up an' set back."

The lean man was humiliated. He smiled at Lockwood and said: "He's a slow eater." He sounded apologetic.

The burly man looked up and around, still holding his poised spoon. He had dark eyes with muddy whites. His expression was not friendly as he growled at the lean man again. "Go outside an' wait, you scrawny son of a bitch."

Half the diners had heard that. Conversation dwindled. The lean man's eyes flicked around the room and back to Lockwood. "He's just joshin'. We josh like that all the time."

Lockwood felt the big man shift on the bench. The large, bearded man's dark eyes neither wavered nor blinked as he looked at the lean man. "I wasn't joshin' an' you know it. You goin' to fire me, Mister Hanson?" He put down his spoon.

The cafe man came along, placed Lockwood's platter in front of him, leaned back, gazing at the other two, got a faint frown, and said: "Gents, this here is a restaurant. If you got a difference, take it outside."

The large man shifted his attention to the cafe man and slowly arose. They were no more than six feet apart. As nearly as Lockwood could tell, the disagreeable, bearded man was not armed. He was big enough not to have to be, at least not in a cafe. He leaned, poked a stiff forefinger into the cafe man's chest, hard. The cafe man stumbled back against his pie table as the large man spoke. There was not a sound in the room. Everyone was looking at the large man when he snarled at the cafe man: "Mind your own business!"

The cafe man was as tall as his antagonist but nowhere nearly as muscled and heavy. However, he had a temper. As he straightened up, his hand came from somewhere with a big knife in it. "Get your butt out of here. Both of you!"

The large man looked from the knife to the cafe man's face and showed strong white teeth when he smiled. "You put down that knife, or I'll make you eat it." As he shifted stance, he bumped Lockwood. He snarled at him too.

Lockwood used a bandanna to wipe his shirt where food had splashed, arose without haste, drew his six-gun, and swung it. The blow drove the large man's hat down over his ears. He collapsed, fell across the counter, upset coffee, broke a sugar bowl, then slid to the floor.

The thin man jumped up and swore at

Lockwood. "He didn't have that comin'. If I had a gun. . . ."

Lockwood turned as he leathered his weapon. "What's your name?" he asked quietly.

The thin man shouldered past to stand looking down. He did not look at Lockwood as he spoke through clenched teeth. "He'll kill you an', if he needs help, I'll do it."

Lockwood seized the thin man by the shoulders, turned him, forced him back against the counter, and continued to lean in as he said it again: "What's your name?" He forced the thin man back until he gasped with pain.

"Charley Hanson."

"What's his name, Charley?"

"Jeff Hanson. He's my brother."

Lockwood released his grip. As the lean man straightened up, he flinched with back pain. His gaze bore into Lockwood. "Wasn't none of your business. Who do you think you are?"

The cafe man spoke before Lockwood could. He was still holding the big knife as he leaned over the counter, looking at the unconscious man. He straightened back and glared at the lean man. "Get his damned carcass outta here an' don't neither of you come in here again. *Get him out of here!*"

The lean man reached for his brother's ankles but could not move the inert weight. Lockwood helped. When they had the man outside on the plank walk, the cafe man's customers crowded out too.

The lean, bewhiskered man named Charley stood stiffly defiant, facing Lockwood. "Mister, you better sprout wings," he said then, as he knelt to use a soiled bandanna to mop at blood from under the pushed-down hat across the unconscious man's cheek.

The onlookers drifted away. Several returned to the cafe, but most of them moved north up the plank walk or crossed the road. The cafe man appeared in the doorway to address Lockwood. "Mister, your grub's gettin' cold."

Later Lockwood appeared in the pool hall doorway. Billy Phelps looked up at him, grinning like a tame ape. "You done it this time, Mister Lockwood. Them's the Hanson brothers. The scrawny one's as treacherous as a damned snake. The one you brained . . . Jeff . . . he's hell on wheels. He's head Indian among the freighters."

Lockwood came in, sat next to Billy Phelps, and gazed soberly at the toes of his boots. "I went in to get somethin' to eat. That's all."

Billy was happy, as though he had good sense of prescience. "If you're in town come dark, you'd better find a real good place to bed down where no one'd look. It was Charley an' another freighter named Dugan forced the town marshal into a fight an' killed him. Say, Mister Lockwood. . . ."

"No!" Lockwood exclaimed. "Get a vigilante committee until you can find another marshal."

He went up to the saloon. His presence dampened all talk. Several loafers at the bar were the same men who had been at the cafe. The barman, a bullet-headed individual with a long, elegantly up-curving dragoon mustache, came along for the order. Lockwood said: "Beer."

The barman stood a moment making his judgment before turning away. He was an inscrutable individual. Rumor had it he had ridden with the Younger brothers. His name was Andrew Lipton. He was old enough to have ridden with the Youngers. In fact, he was old enough to have been in the war, but he did not carry an ounce of surplus flesh, and his pale gaze was stone-steady. When he returned, he picked up the five-cent piece, paused just long enough to provide Lockwood an opportunity to talk if he was of a mind, and walked away when

Lockwood ignored him.

When he got back to the rooming house, the proprietor was sitting in the same rocker she'd used the previous night. She had been watching Lockwood's progress after he left the saloon. When he reached the porch, the woman did as she'd done before — she patted the seat of the chair beside her.

Lockwood sat, pushed out his legs, and gazed toward the lower end of town. Bertha Bradley broke the silence between them. "You'd have done better to shoot him, Mister Lockwood."

"He wasn't armed."

She shocked him this night as she had an earlier night. "You should have shot him anyway." The woman turned her head. "Have you been east of town?"

"No."

"There's a grove of cottonwoods over there an' a runnin' spring. That's where the freighters camp. You can count on at least three, four wagons over there every year from spring through autumn. Countin' swampers that'd be no less than six, eight men." She continued to study Lockwood who was facing in a different direction. "Maybe you shouldn't have settled with Jeff. You should've just set and listened. Them two argue and cuss each other just naturally.

It would have blown over. It always has. The big one just naturally picks on the skinny one."

Lockwood looked at the older woman. "How was I to know? That big feller with the face-feathers spilled food on me. Then he growled somethin' about me being in his way."

Bertha nodded sagely. They were all the same, four or forty. Hair-triggered. She rocked a moment. "I'd say Jeff had it coming. Most folks around town would agree with me. He's a mean, troublesome son of a bitch."

Lockwood was shocked again. Women, even dance-hall girls, didn't use that kind of language.

"But, Mister Lockwood, it wasn't just takin' offense. The Hansons and their friends will take it out on the town. That's how we lost our last town marshal. He called two drunk freighters. They buried him two days later." Bertha stopped rocking. "That was about three weeks ago."

Lockwood was gazing steadily at her. There was no way to misunderstand what she was hinting. "It's a fair-size town," he told her. "Six or eight freighters don't amount to an army, ma'am."

She nodded about that. "We'll do what

we can, Mister Lockwood. You can count on that. What I'm sayin' is that it don't seem right that you get into a fight, and the rest of us got to take the consequences."

Lockwood stood up, told her good night, and went inside.

Chapter Three

DERBY

A man had a right to be resentful. It wasn't his town, and he hadn't started that fight. It was springtime, and by his reckoning he still had a long way to go. When he entered the cafe, all conversation stopped. Men kept their heads lowered over breakfast — all but the nondescript cafe man with the skin darker than most and the steady gaze. He smiled as he took Lockwood's order, went to his cooking area, and whistled some vaguely familiar tune.

As the man was placing the platter in front of Lockwood, their eyes met. The cafe man slowly winked before walking away. Lockwood was not heartened. He had one friend in Derby but that would last only until the cafe man heard that Lockwood had saddled up and ridden on. He ate, placed silver beside the plate, arose, nodded to the cafe man who nodded back, and walked out of the cafe.

There were four of them. One had a rag around his head which made his old hat sit high. Two he had never seen before, but he recognized the big burly man and his brother before the door had closed behind him. Three of them had Winchesters as well as belt guns. Skinny Charley had just his six-gun.

They blocked his access, stood like statues staring at Lockwood. Somewhere northward someone slammed a door. Across the road in front of the jailhouse two old men who had been absorbing sunlight on a wall bench arose and walked away.

A light buggy with a fringed top passed, picked up speed, and swerved toward the east plank walk up in front of the bank. A pair of riders coming from the south on loose reins were talking. One of them said something sharp. Both men briefly halted then turned back the way they had come.

Up at the rooming house a dowdy graying woman was standing on the porch as though she had taken root. That stone-faced barman with the luxurious dragoon mustache was out front wearing his apron looking southward. There were other onlookers behind windows, in recessed doorways. Most of them had seen the four freighters, armed to the gills, walking toward the cafe. Down at the smithy someone took measured strikes at a hot horseshoe atop an anvil. At least someone in Derby had no inkling of the drama in front of the cafe, but the cafe man in the cafe had seen those four freighters out front with Winchesters, and he darted past an old rug which separated his living area from the kitchen. He moved with surprising agility for a man who was twenty years older than he looked.

When he came back carrying a big old horse pistol, Army issue, his diners stared and froze where they sat. The cafe man went hurriedly to his alley door, turned north to the first dog-trot between buildings, and came up to the front roadway about a hundred feet north. He got there just in time to hear Jeff Hanson call Lockwood every fighting name he knew.

If Lockwood had a chance, it had to be in the nature of a miracle. He was fast and deadly; he was also hopelessly out-numbered at about six feet. Two of the freighters raised the Winchesters belt-buckle high. Lockwood had to fight. He watched Jeff Hanson and sneered.

"I heard around town you gents fight like coyotes . . . four to one or better."

The big bearded man's dark eyes with the muddy whites did not blink. "You hit me from behind," he said.

Lockwood's answer to that was simple.

"Walk out into the roadway. Man to man . . . you son of a bitch."

Charley cursed Lockwood. "Who you callin' a son of a bitch . . . *you* son of a bitch!"

Jeff was tipping his Winchester when a solitary loud gunshot came from northward. The man next to Jeff was punched sideways. He bumped the other man with the leveled Winchester. That man pulled the trigger. His bullet shattered wooden siding as it went through the front wall of the cafe. Inside, men squawked and ducked.

Charley Hanson jumped as though he had been shot and swung half around looking for the killer of the freighter. At that moment Lockwood drew and fired point-blank. The big man's Winchester went off skyward as he was knocked off the plank walk into the street. His brother yelped, swung back, and clawed at his hip holster. Charley was fast. Lockwood only had to turn his wrist, cock, and squeeze the trigger, yet even so both hand guns exploded almost simultaneously. Charley's speed was surprising, but his aim was not as good. His bullet struck Lockwood across the upper part of his left leg. Impact made Lockwood fall, but Charley would never use his fast gun again. He had been hit squarely in the center of the brisket. Like his brother, he was dead before he fell off the plank walk.

Lockwood swung his six-gun with the hammer full back. The surviving freighter dropped his weapon, shoved both hands high, and yelled like a wounded varmint.

People appeared at a safe distance. One of those two old gummers who had discreetly left the bench across the road, which would have been in the line of fire, nudged the other one and said: "That there youngster could take care of himself in a nest of rattlers."

While the bold approached the cafe with its splintered front, Lockwood told the surviving freighter to shed his hand gun and get face forward against the cafe. The freighter obeyed, but he was whining. "You dassn't shoot a man in the back with everyone watchin'."

Lockwood sat down with his feet in the roadway. Now, finally, the pain came. He ground his teeth, leathered his weapon, saw the two old men, and called to them. "Is there a doctor in Derby?"

There was no medical practitioner and never had been, but there was a combination veterinarian and midwife. She was bearing down on Lockwood from the upper end of town where her rooming house was, unkempt gray hair awry, stride long and purposeful. She had a small satchel in one hand.

Inside the cafe diners, who had long since lost whatever appetite they'd had, watched the cafe man return with that big old horse pistol at his side. He neither looked at them nor spoke. He returned to his living quarters, was back there only a moment, then reappeared wearing his apron. He went behind the counter, considered his customers, and said: "I never left. You boys'll swear to that. I hid behind the counter." He went after the coffee pot, wordlessly refilled every cup, put the pot aside, and went to open his roadway door and look out.

Bertha looked up at him. "Lend me a hand, Stuart." As the cafe man came over and knelt, Bertha said: "Pull that belt as tight as you can get it."

They stopped the bleeding with Lockwood looking down as though this was being done to someone else, not to him. He didn't feel sick. He felt dizzy. His vision was blurry.

Bertha poured something from a small bottle, held it up, and told Lockwood to drink, which he did. Within minutes there was no pain. His vision was still blurry, but his body gradually felt warm, comfortable, and relaxed.

The blacksmith's helper, a powerful young

man with a mop of unruly fair hair, got on one side of Lockwood. Bertha was on the other side as they began the long walk up the middle of the roadway to the rooming house.

Two men, the saloonman with bald head and handsome dragoon mustache wearing frilly lavender sleeve-garters, the other pudgy with pants and coat that matched, watched the survivor being punched over to the jail-house to be locked up, as the other men hoisted the corpses heading for the shed behind the abstract office where the man who dealt in deeds for land did embalming on the side.

The saloonman, impassive as ever, quietly told the pudgy man he'd never seen the like. Four against one and three were killed, one gave up whining like a baby, and the victim getting off with nothing more than a slashed leg.

The pudgy man nodded, mopped his face, and hurried back to the bank where a raw-boned woman with tanned skin and testy blue eyes, wearing a split riding skirt, Mex spurs with silver inlay, was sitting beside a desk waiting. When the pudgy man returned, she said: "Well, what was it this time?"

"Four freighters braced a cowboy I never

saw before in front of the cafe."

"And . . . ?"

"Miz Barlow, you won't believe it. He shot three, got hit in the leg. Bertha's takin' him up to her place."

"You said four freighters, Homer."

"They locked one up in the jailhouse."

"What was it about?"

"I got no idea."

The rawboned woman stood up. "When you find out, let me know," she said, walked out, hoisted the tether-weight, got into the fringe-topped buggy with it, talked up the buggy mare, and drove northward out of town without looking right or left.

Bertha saw her pass as she and the blacksmith's helper were getting Lockwood through the door. By the time they got him to his room, he was bleeding again. They put him on the bed, and he smiled at them, speaking like a man with a swollen tongue. "I'm obliged. I'll be fine. Just rest a little."

Bertha responded gruffly. "Humph!" She looked at the stalwart blacksmith's helper. "That's the laudanum talking. Thanks for your help."

"I can stay if you want, Miz Bradley."

"No. You go on. I can manage. Lord knows, I've been through things like this before. Thanks, son. Tell Ezra, when you get back to the smithy, to set someone watchin' that one in the jailhouse. Tell him what happened. Tell him sure-Lord those freighters out yonder aren't goin' to like this."

The young man nodded about that. The blacksmith wouldn't really have to be told. Neither would anyone else in town. It might take a while for the shock of what had happened in front of the cafe to reach the men at the freighters' camp, but no one doubted what would happen when that happened.

Bertha had a struggle getting Lockwood undressed and bathed. He drifted in and out of awareness and, when he was out of it, he fought to protect his privacy. No matter how hard she argued to convince him that he wasn't the first male she'd given an all-over bath to, he did not even try to cooperate.

Only on the second day, when he was rational and willing to eat, did she mention the birthmark. He passed it off as he'd always done, with a shrug. Bertha had no reason to press the discussion. She had seen birthmarks before, if not often or very many. Birthmarks were not that common. His, she told him, looked like a three-quarter moon. He said he'd been told it resembled a horseshoe. She made no issue — it could look like a horseshoe but with very wide heels.

Her concern was the leg wound. She had cleaned and disinfected it as best she could. The leg swelled until it was twice as large as it normally was, and it was very painful, particularly when Lockwood shifted position. But she told him each morning she was satisfied, that so far there was no sullen red which would indicate infection.

On the fifth day, when she entered the room, he looked quizzically at her. "I'm not exactly sure what happened, but I'd swear I heard someone shoot from up the plank walk somewhere."

She had heard the same version of the fight from a dozen people and, while it had varied slightly with each telling, it never varied about Lockwood's killing all three freighters.

They sat one evening with the window open. Springtime was yielding to summer. There were hot days, but as yet summer had not firmed its grip, and there were also occasional pleasant cool days. She had fed him earlier. He asked her to get the makings from his shirt pocket, which she did and watched him roll and light a smoke. When he removed the cigarette, he nodded toward the holstered six-gun hanging by the shell belt from a hook on the back of the door.

"There's two empty casings, Miz Bradley."

She did not understand the innuendo for a moment, then she frowned. "You're tellin' me you only shot twice?"

"Yes'm."

She turned to look at the hanging gun belt. "Mister Lockwood, there was three dead freighters."

He nodded. "I know that."

She stared at the hands in her lap for a moment before raising her eyes. "It doesn't make sense."

"It does if someone else fired that first shot. It's come back to me that, when I remember back, someone did, and they fired from up north, somewhere south of the bank maybe."

"Do you have friends, Mister Lockwood?"

He grinned crookedly at her. "That day I sure did. But no, I can't say I've made any particular friends in Derby." He checked himself up for a moment before asking her about the cafe man. She told him what she knew. "He came here about six, seven years back. There was a woman had the cafe before that. Margaret Flannery. She and Ike Hightower, one of the stage drivers, was seein' each other every time he came through. When Stuart Bentley came to town, she sold out to him." Bertha faintly smiled. "Men cooks didn't make much of a dent in a place where folks always figured only women could cook. But he hung on, an' for a fact Stuart is a good cook. He told me one time he's from the hills of Arkansas. He was a Rebel soldier."

"He don't look old enough for that," Lockwood said, and the dowdy but shrewd-eyed older woman agreed. "He doesn't for a fact. We got to be good friends. He told me one time he killed a loud-mouthed Texan in a knife fight. I can tell you this, Mister Lockwood, he's a typical Secesh . . . good friend if he likes you, careful not to say the wrong thing, quick to take offense if someone says the wrong thing. My husband was from the South. They're just naturally quick tempered." She paused to look steadily at Lockwood. "You've eaten there?"

He nodded. "Since I came to Derby."

"Did you and Stuart get friendly?"

He thought about that and remembered something that fit the man she had described. "Well, not exactly friendly, but the day I had a tussle with the Hansons, that big one had threatened the cafe man, who pulled a knife on him. That's when I hit the big feller over the head."

Bertha was sagely nodding before Lockwood finished speaking. "You have a friend, Mister Lockwood. Stuart would remember something like that. My husband was the same way."

Lockwood gazed at his holstered Colt, slowly returned his gaze to the woman, and gently wagged his head. After she departed, he limped to the only window in his room and stood gazing southward down through town. It was getting along toward the end of the day. There were men converging on the cafe.

The next morning, when Bertha Bradley appeared, Lockwood had dressed himself. She stopped in the doorway, scowling. "If you get on a horse, Mister Lockwood, you won't get a mile before it'll commence to bleed." She closed the door at her back and stood in front of it. "I know. Men get restless. My husband wouldn't stay in bed even when he was too sick to sit up. You aren't ready yet. You've got to keep off that leg as much as you can for another week . . . at the least. A horse'll jar the scabs loose."

He smiled at her. "How about a little walk?"

She continued to scowl but not as fiercely. "How far?"

"Just down through town a ways and back."

"Wait, I got to comb my hair," she told him and turned to open the door.

He stopped her. "Alone, Miz Bradley. If I go walkin' with you hangin' on like I'm a little kid. . . ."

She interrupted him with a snort. "Men! Men and their damned pride! That's what's filled half the graveyards in this country! All right, go ahead, but if you get on a horse or even walk the full length of town, don't come cryin' to me if it's bleeding when you get back." She stamped out of the room and slammed the door after herself.

The leg was sound enough. He'd used it to and from the outhouse for several days. As he walked out onto the verandah and stood watching foot and horse traffic for a moment or two, the sun reached him. It was hot but pleasant. He took down a big breath and started walking — with a limp, because there was still pain with movement but not enough to make him more than passingly conscious of it. He went down as far as the bench in front of the jailhouse, which was across from the cafe, sat down, and nodded to the pair of tobacco-chewing old gummers who were also sitting there. They nodded gravely back, exchanged a look before one of them said: "Good to see you up 'n' around. That was one hell of a fight. We was settin' over here until it looked like stray bullets might come this way."

Lockwood eased both legs out, one hurt but not very much. "You gents saw the whole thing?"

They both nodded. One had to jettison brown juice so the other one said, "Right from when we seen them four freighters coming south from up by the saloon. One of 'em only had his belt gun. The others had Winchesters. Seen everythin' as clear as day. You did right well, considerin' the odds. Real well."

Lockwood was gazing across the road when he asked his next question. "Who fired the first shot?"

One old man raised a scrawny arm and shifted his cud before replying. "It come from that dog-trot just south of the bank. Black powder gun." He dropped the arm as his companion solemnly nodded. "Black powder. I ain't seen a black powder gun fired in ten years."

"Did you see who fired?"

The old men shook their heads almost in unison. One spat before speaking. "I seen the gun but only for a glimpse, then whoever was in the dog-trot yanked it back." He squinted both eyes in thought and chewed for a moment before speaking again. "Do you know the feller who owns the saloon? He was out front lookin' down this way. If anyone seen that feller in the dog-trot, it'd be him."

Lockwood thanked the old gaffers and limped across the road on his way northward to the saloon.

Chapter Four

A GATHERING STORM

Quite a few of the Irish had saloons. It was a business that combined things dear to hearts from the Auld Sod — conviviality, drink, gossip, a mite of gambling, and belly laughter. But Andrew Lipton, the barman, was neither Irish nor convivial. He was mostly impassive and taciturn, things that would not have ordinarily encouraged business, but he served good whiskey — his own particular variety of home brew made with painstaking attention to ingredients — and his saloon was large with a big iron stove to keep the place warm in winter.

He did not do much business mornings, but later in the day and evenings he did. When Lockwood limped in, the proprietor was leaning on the bar with a cup of coffee, spectacles down his nose, reading a newspaper someone had left at a poker table the night before.

He peered over the top of his glasses, folded the newspaper, shoved it on the backbar shelf, and said: "Morning. What'll you have?"

Lockwood leaned, hoisted his injured leg to the brass rail, settled most of his weight on the other leg, and said: "Coffee."

Lipton hadn't expected that. Saloons sold liquor. Cafes sold coffee. Lockwood nodded in the direction of the speckle-ware pot and placed two-bits in silver atop the counter. Lipton went over to fill a cup, wordlessly placed it in front of his only bar customer, and pocketed the quarter dollar.

They regarded each other in silence. Lockwood half drained the cup and continued to lean, looking at the bald man with the formidable dragoon mustache and lavender sleeve-garters.

Lipton spoke finally, since it seemed his customer was not going to. "That was a messy business down yonder, Mister Lockwood."

His customer drained the cup and shoved it aside, looking directly at the saloonman. "Who fired the first shot?"

Lipton raised a bar rag from its fold in his apron, looked only at what he was doing as he made a wide swab of the countertop. "All I saw was a long-barreled pistol, and the smoke after it was fired."

"Where was he?"

"In that dog-trot south of the bank."

"Any idea who he was?"

Lipton made another swipe over his bar top before speaking. "It was a black-powder gun. I haven't seen one of those in years."

"Any idea?"

Andrew Lipton's expressionless gaze rested on Lockwood. "Mister, you survived . . . them four didn't . . . three permanently. If I was you, I'd be content to count my blessings."

Lockwood leaned both forearms on the counter, his gaze steadily bearing on the bald man with the frilly sleeve garters. "Mind tellin' me your name?"

"Andrew Lipton."

"Mister Lipton . . . who was he!"

Lipton took the empty cup back, refilled it, refilled his own cup, and returned, his face impassive. "I told you . . . all I saw was the gun. I didn't see it until he fired, then I only had a glimpse for maybe two, three seconds."

Lockwood considered the coffee. He wasn't much of a coffee man. One or two cups a day. He pushed the cup aside. There was something going on here. He reared back, rolled a smoke, spilt tobacco atop the bar, lighted up, and trickled smoke through which he looked unwaveringly at the saloonman.

Lipton's face showed nothing, but once or

twice his gaze wavered. Lockwood wasn't just some rangeman who wore a gun. He had shot it out with four men, killed two who had all the edge men usually needed to kill someone. Lipton spoke in an inflectionless tone. "You wouldn't remember the war."

"I remember," Lockwood said. "I was a kid, but I remember. What about it?"

"U. S. troops was armed with a horse-pistol like folks don't use any more. They used black powder. When enough men was firing, you couldn't see the enemy. It didn't help that he was doing the same thing."

Lockwood reconsidered, drank some coffee, put the cup aside, and was patient. He'd encountered them before, old warriors. Once they got cranked up, it took a while before they ran down.

"The Secesh had pretty much the same pistols. Ours was government-issue, as alike as peas in a pod. Secesh hand guns seemed mostly to be weapons from home. There was everything from smooth-bore muskets their granddaddies had used to modern pistols like was issued officers of the Union."

Lockwood was beginning to get a glimmer. He interrupted to ask if Mr. Lipton had been an officer. The reply he got was made in the only change in an otherwise toneless monologue. "Second Company, First Minnesota Sharpshooters," the voice faltered, then resumed in almost a whisper. "Eighty percent casualties in eighteen minutes at Gettysburg." Lipton's gaze wandered and returned. "That gun had the long underpinning in brass many Secesh used, Mister Lockwood. That's all I can tell you."

Lipton reached for his coffee cup, drained it, put it down, and looked impassively at Lockwood without saying another word. As Lockwood straightened back, easing his sore leg gently to the floor, he shook his head. "In eighteen minutes? Mister Lipton, that's not war, that's massacre."

Andrew Lipton stood gazing at the roadway doors long after they had stopped moving following Lockwood's departure. An old man, sitting outside in front of a roadway window watching traffic, turned. "You was on the wrong side, Andrew. We grew up barkin' squirrels in trees at thirty yards with them black-powder guns."

Heat was bearing down. Horse traffic had lessened. The old men on the bench in front of the jailhouse were gone and in their place was a massive older man wearing a worn old split muleskin shoeing apron. Ezra Evans, the town blacksmith.

He watched Lockwood limping in the direction of the cafe, shook his head slightly, and marveled for the tenth time how any man could have survived what that stranger had lived through.

It was too early for dinnertime. The cafe man was leaning down on his counter, conversing with the bewhiskered livery man who was built like a gorilla. For a fact Bertha had been right. About all that was visible was a pair of little eyes, a nose, and a mouth when the livery man spoke.

The cafe man ambled over where Lockwood sat, nodded pleasantly, and said: "You're in luck today, partner. I bought three bags of prairie chickens off some pothunters. They're in the oven right now. Give or take fifteen minutes an' I'll set a meal before you a man can't get short of Cincinnati."

Lockwood watched the dark-skinned, testy-eyed man draw off his coffee. Lockwood didn't touch it. He looked down where the bear of a livery man was scarfing up food like he hadn't eaten in a week, lowered his voice as he said, "You haven't patched the front wall yet."

The cafe man threw a glance in the direction of the splintered wood and nodded. "In time, friend. I got more important things to do. You want pie with them prairie chickens?

I fresh baked two from crab apples. They're a mite tart, but they tell me too much sweets ain't good for a man."

The cafe man's gaze showed mild inward uneasiness. Lockwood took advantage of that. As he addressed the cafe man, he used his name. "Mister Bentley, I'm obliged."

"For what?"

Lockwood waited until the livery man had paid and departed before replying. "For bein' in that dog-trot."

Stuart Bentley showed a faint red stain under his dark hide, but he was a direct man with a simple philosophy about life, how to live it, how to react to statements like the one Lockwood had made. "I missed that big son of a bitch. He's the one I wanted. My gun's too old." A flicker of ironic amusement showed briefly in the cafe man's eyes. "Maybe so'm I, but for a fact him an' the feller I hit was too close together."

Lockwood showed a thin, faint smile. "I'm obliged anyway. Is that prairie chicken about done?"

Bertha was sitting on the verandah in pleasant shade, knitting needles rattling like the noise of an agitated woodpecker, when Lockwood limped up, swung a chair, and sat down.

Bertha said: "Well!"

"I didn't fire the first shot," Lockwood said and felt her staring at him. In order to ward off her next question, he also said: "You were right. They are a quick-tempered lot. They never forget an insult nor a helpin' hand."

The knitting needles began rattling again. She did not say a word until he rolled and lighted a smoke. "Did the leg bleed?" Before he could answer, she jerked her head in the direction of the door behind them. "Get back in bed. I'll be along directly. If it opened up, I'll make a fresh bandage. I saw you talk to those old men out front of the jailhouse, then go up to Andy Lipton's place, then down to the cafe."

Lockwood did something which was out of character for him, as he arose favoring his leg. He stooped, kissed Bertha on the cheek, and went inside.

She stopped knitting, stopped rocking, looked southward toward the far end of town with misty eyes. *Men!* They make a woman mad enough to bite the front end of a rattler one moment and make them melt inside the next moment. This one had upset her from the first time she'd seen him. He looked enough like her dead husband to be his younger brother. If there was a God, he sure-Lord had a faulty sense of what folks needed and what they didn't need. Resurrecting memories they didn't need!

By late afternoon it was hot with no air stirring and some clouds with dirty gray edgings were passing in long streamers. At times they obscured the sun, but shade in hot weather, particularly when it was accompanied with clouds like that, might obscure the sun yet do nothing to alleviate the heat.

Lockwood napped and sweated. He had an unpleasant dream going back to early spring. It wasn't the first time, wouldn't be the last time. Perhaps even some years ahead it would be very vivid, more so than at other times, almost as though some part of the dream was trying to find him, trying to touch him.

He was awakened by the door opening and closing. Bertha was standing there. She didn't say a word as she came close, bent, and examined the bandage. She reared back, looking disgusted. "I told you it'd open. I'll get fresh bandaging." At the door she looked back, shook her head, and departed.

Lockwood had to sit up to see the cloth. There was a small spot of blood that had soaked through. Actually the leg had begun to hurt less after his hike around town.

When Bertha returned, she had a companion, another woman. This one was taller with dark hair and hints of silver above the ears. She was as flat-chested as a man, on the rawboned side with a square jaw, and a no-nonsense look in her eyes.

Bertha introduced them. "Mister Lockwood, this here is Lady Barlow. Miz Barlow, this here is Cuff Lockwood."

The woman barely inclined her head. Lockwood did better. He smiled, but something in the back of his brain was sending alarm signals.

Bertha went to work on the leg as the hard-eyed woman addressed Lockwood. Her style was brusque, but her voice was pleasant. "Bertha told me you'd be another few weeks healing." She paused. "I own Barlow ranch northeast of town. I keep three year-round riders and a foreman. He gave me notice day before yesterday." She paused again. "He's been with the ranch since years before my husband died. I didn't expect it. He said when a man reaches his age it's time to think about movin' into town, finding somethin' to do where a person can stay cool in summer and warm in winter."

Bertha growled. "Lift the leg. Higher. Now hold it like that."

The steely-eyed woman was only momentarily distracted. "I need a replacement,

Mister Lockwood."

He studied her. "Sounds like you do, Miz Barlow."

"Would you be interested?"

His eyes widened a fraction. To his knowledge he'd never seen the woman before, nor had she seen him. Bertha cleared something up by saying, "I told her you were a stockman. The whole town knows you're capable enough, Mister Lockwood."

He sorted through some vague thoughts before speaking. "Miz Barlow, you don't know me from Adam's off ox."

"I know enough, Mister Lockwood. You handled yourself well in front of the cafe some time back."

He scowled faintly. "That didn't have anythin' to do with ramroddin' a cattle outfit, ma'am."

The steely eyes never wavered. "I'll take a chance, Mister Lockwood. I'm a fair judge of men."

Bertha finished with the bandaging, looked Lockwood straight in the eyes, and said: "No more walkin' around town until it's plumb healed. Maybe two, three weeks."

He nodded about that and spoke again to the whipcord-built woman with the claw-hammer jaw. "You don't want to wait a month."

She already knew from Bertha how much longer his recovery might take. "My foreman won't quit until I get a replacement. We've agreed on that. Think about it. We'll talk again."

After the woman left, Lockwood swung around, planted both feet firmly, and stood up. The injured leg hardly hurt. He made a smoke and stood by the window. The roadway was busy as usual. Down in front of the jailhouse several men were solemnly talking. One was pudgy with thinning hair. His back was to Lockwood. One whose face he could see owned the mercantile which had seemed to Lockwood to be the most successful business in Derby. There were two other men he couldn't see clearly.

Otherwise the scene was about as it usually was, except for one thing. Over in front of Lipton's water hole there were three heavily armed men whose general appearance indicated they were probably freighters.

They were loafing over there, watching traffic, smoking or chewing, not having much to say to each other. When another man dressed about the same emerged from the saloon, the four of them went to the tie rack, got astride, and rode out of town northward. Lockwood could not see where they left the road riding eastward.

Bertha returned with a bowl as large as the ones used for soup, except that this one had a handle which, technically anyway, made it a cup. It was full to the brim of wonderfully aromatic beef broth. She handed it to Lockwood as she said, "That's really her first name. Lady. Drink it, it's not too hot. I've known her fifteen, eighteen years. She runs that outfit with no frills, an' she's done real well since her husband died. Mister Lockwood, when you're able, you could do a lot worse'n what she offered."

He lowered the cup, motioned Bertha to the only chair, sat on the edge of the bed, and cocked his head at her. "It don't make sense. For all she knows I can't even make a decent gate tally let alone run a cow outfit."

"Like she told you, she's a good judge of men."

He drank more broth before speaking again. "Remember? I just stopped in Derby on my way south."

She had an answer for that too. "The last day or two there's been freighters in town. Strangers. Mostly folks know the ones that've been hauling us supplies over the years." She put her head slightly to one side. "In case you've wondered why they haven't struck back, it's because it takes a while for them to contact their friends and more time for their friends to get here."

"Now they're here?"

"Seems that way. Homer Westphal, who manages Lady Barlow's bank, the man who runs the mercantile, and some others around town know for a fact more freighters are in camp out yonder than there's any reason for it."

Lockwood remembered the men down in front of the jailhouse. He finished the broth, leaned to hand her the bowl, and straightened back, gazing at her. "If you know trouble's coming, Bertha, get ready for it. Round up the men and be ready."

She loosened in the chair, regarding him. "They're ready, Mister Lockwood. The way they feel about it, you shot it out with four of them. They'll want your hide most of all. Folks believe, since it's your war as much as theirs, you'd ought to take the lead."

He sat in nonplused silence, looking at her. Eventually he swung his gaze to the window where he could see down through town. He should have dragged himself astride after the gunfight in front of the cafe and ridden on, bleeding or not.

He looked back at her. She sat there like a dowdy Buddha watching everything he did. "Do you think that's fair?" he asked.

She answered first without speaking, just slowly bobbing her head up and down. "I think it is, so does Lady Barlow."

He stared. "What's she got to do with this?"

"It's her bank. Mister Lockwood, wild-eyed freighters ridin' roughshod might fire the town. Sure as hell the worst of them would raid the bank, take all the savings of folks like me, as well as her money."

He arose to go stand with his back to her, looking southward. For a town about to be raided, Derby looked uncommonly indifferent to peril.

"Mister Lockwood, Lady said she'd send riders if things look bad."

He turned. "Let . . . Lady . . . ramrod the fight, Bertha. Seems to me she's more man than woman."

Bertha was not the least perturbed by his exasperation. As always she had a practical answer. "It'd never work. For one thing she's not real well liked in town. For another . . . and I know how this is . . . not a man in Derby would take orders from a woman."

"Where's the nearest Army post?"

"Eighty miles south, down over the border in Colorado. If we had a telegraph, which we don't have, an' if they got the story by suppertime tonight, they couldn't get up here for at the very least two days. More likely three, four days."

He did not mention the obvious: When would the freighters hoorawh the town?

Bertha arose, swept a careless hand over her unruly hair, and went to the door. From over there she said: "They'll come to see you tonight."

"Who will?"

"The mercantile owner, the blacksmith, the feller who does the abstract and undertaking, Stuart Bentley from the cafe . . . I'll get you a decent dinner."

This time, when Bertha departed, she closed the door so gently it made almost no noise.

Chapter Five

A NEWCOMER

It rained in the night. By morning it was coming down like a fat cow peeing on a flat rock but, before the first drops fell, Lockwood had the visitors Bertha had warned him about. The only one he knew well enough to nod at was the cafe man who introduced the others. Lockwood had a hazy recollection of the pudgy man, but the blacksmith and store owner were strangers.

He was offered a cigar, which he declined. He liked cigars, but they didn't like him. The mercantile proprietor was a paunchy individual sporting a massive gold chain across his middle. He hadn't been outside much, and his skin was as soft as a baby's bottom. He was evidently the appointed spokesman and was smooth and genial as he put the town's case before Lockwood, who perched on the edge of his bed fully clothed, fed, and fuming.

It was essentially the same argument Bertha had offered, not once but twice. Lockwood had started the trouble. It was his duty to help the town finish it. When he would have interrupted, the portly merchant with the soft, lineless skin held up a hand.

"Mister Lockwood, we organized a vigilance committee. Me 'n' the gents with me tonight, plus seven other fellers around town. What we figure is that they'll use the excuse of takin' that scoundrel you got at the jailhouse back with them. An' we figure whether we hand him over or not, they'll roust the town. If we cave in, they'll start a fight over us holdin' their friend. You understand?"

Lockwood understood. He had understood moments after the merchant had started speaking. He knew the moment he stated his reason for being in their town, and how he'd been goaded into the fight in front of the cafe, and finally that he'd been on his way south, they were going to say what Bertha had said — twice. Whatever the underlying causes for mutual dislike between townsmen and freighters, he had started the ball rolling by killing three of the freighters. And that had precipitated the fight certain to come. Right now it didn't matter that he'd killed two, not three.

He rolled and lit a smoke with the four men watching. The blacksmith was tired of standing and went after three chairs. In his absence Lockwood's particular — and only — friend in Derby spoke in his half drawl, half twang. One time he sounded like someone with a mouth full of mush; another time he had a faint sing-song lilt to his conversation. This time it was the sing-song lilt.

"We can buck 'em, Mister Lockwood. There's plenty of us. But you'd ought to remember it's you they want in particular, if they got to burn down the town to get you. None of us shot their friends. If they get you, you got any idea what they'll do? Tie your arms an' legs, hang you in the middle of town for everyone to watch you strangle. Mister Lockwood, with them kind, that'll only be openers." The cafe man paused, took a deep breath, and said his clincher. "An' you can't ride. Not without bustin' that leg loose and most likely bleedin' to death."

Lockwood considered each of them in turn. With the possible exception of the baby-faced store keeper they looked capable. He knew for a fact the cafe man was, and he might have wagered his life on the blacksmith, he looked resolute enough. He laughed hollowly. If he weathered this tussle like he'd weathered the one in front of the cafe, he could still make it down to New Mexico or somewhere it didn't snow. He gazed out the window with the men watching him as silent as stones. And if he didn't weather this mess any better than he'd weathered the other fight, he could end up on his back being fussed over by Bertha right up until it snowed.

The cafe man broke the silence. "We got some outside volunteer help."

Lockwood faced back toward them. "So I heard. Miz Barlow's riders."

"They're good men," the pudgy banker said. "They been in the country a fair spell. If you figure we should, we can send for them."

Lockwood settled his gaze on the pudgy man. If *you* figure . . . ? Their minds had been made up before they came to the rooming house. He continued his regard of the pudgy man as he said: "Not yet. For the time bein' you gents could go around through town and make damned sure every man who's got a gun has ammunition to go with it."

Every one of their faces showed relief. The cafe man looked downright enthusiastic; those old Rebels had been good fighters and occasionally good leaders. He didn't tell them he'd seen freighters loafing in front of the saloon until one of their friends emerged. If he had made an insinuation, there would have been an argument, probably with all four of them swearing to high heaven Andrew Lipton disliked freighters as well as the others did, and maybe he did. And maybe he didn't. Being committed, finally, Lockwood chose not to cause any distractions.

After the Derby delegation departed, Bertha appeared in the doorway. For once she'd done something with her hair. It looked neater than usual, but what Bertha required was a lot more than neat hair. She had probably learned that corral-yard language from her late husband. She said: "Are you in or out?"

Lockwood's reply was not enthusiastic. "In."

She departed only to return in minutes with a bottle of whiskey and two small glasses. Lockwood solemnly watched her fill the glasses, accepted one, and did not smile when she said: "I knew you'd do it. So did Lady Barlow."

He downed the liquor, turned the jolt glass wrong-side up on the windowsill, and fished for his makings. Lady Barlow had nothing to do with it. He lit up, trickled smoke, and said: "Bertha, I don't like any of this."

"Neither does anyone else, Mister Lockwood, but we didn't start it."

He thought he'd better get used to hearing

that and looked at the dowdy older woman. "You need the Army. I'm not a soldier an' never have been one."

"Folks considered that, but what we *know* is that they're gatherin' out yonder an', when they get ready, if the soldiers aren't here, they'd never get here in time."

He opened the window. It was beginning to rain, softly, gently but with unmistakable persistence. While his back was to her, Bertha had another jolt. She took the bottle with her and closed the door after herself.

Lockwood bedded down listening to rain, which normally was pleasant and soothing, but not this night.

In the morning the air smelled wet. It had rained all night and was still raining as Lockwood arose, dressed, and went out back to shave with cold water and lye soap which did not lather. He returned from the wash house, got his hat, buckled his shell belt and holstered Colt, and started for the cafe.

The roadbed was soggy. Derby was shrouded in dismal gray. There was no traffic and stove smoke arose here and there. The cafe had fewer breakfast customers than usual, and the prevailing mood was in keeping with the weather outside. The cafe man brought the only thing he fed folks for breakfast, put the platter in front of Lockwood, did not smile, leaned low and said, "See that feller with the black hat? He come from the freighter camp."

Before Lockwood could ask how the cafe man knew this, he was called away by a diner whose coffee cup was empty.

The man with the black hat did not look like a freighter. He wore a rangeman's attire, faded work shirt of blue and trousers nearly as worn and colorless. He was young with averted eyes, a wide, thin mouth with no beard, not even a mustache. His hair had not been neglected either. He looked like he could possibly be a traveling peddler or maybe one of those itinerant tooth-pullers who passed through every town occasionally.

Because he was seated, Lockwood could not see whether he wore a shell belt and weapon. When the cafe man came back, Lockwood caught his eyes. When the cafe man had gotten rid of two platters of breakfast, he returned and leaned down.

"He don't look like a freighter, Stuart."

"All I know is that he come ridin' in from the cottonwood camp. I was out back filling a trash barrel and watched him. He come straight as an arrer from the direction of the cottonwood camp."

The cafe man hurried to his kitchen where he had meat cooking in an iron fry-pan.

When he came back, he had nothing to say, but he rolled his eyes before moving away.

The rainfall increased. It made a dull, steady sound on the roof of the cafe. A diner raised his head, listened, growled something to the man on his right, and went back to eating. Lockwood thought the dark-hatted man was dawdling through his breakfast. Lockwood didn't. He'd been hungry when he bedded down last night.

One by one the diners departed. Each time someone opened the roadway door, dampness and chilly wind came in. When there were only four diners at the counter, the stranger with the black hat finished, pushed his platter away, pulled in his coffee cup, and raised his face. The cafe man was behind the old rug that served as a door in his cooking area. He watched the stranger as the man turned enough to see Lockwood eating. As the stranger straightened, he caught a glimpse of the watching cafe man.

As though he had seen nothing to cause worry, he drained his cup and also pushed it aside. Another replete diner left. There were now two diners, and Lockwood at the counter. Lockwood was finishing his meal as he reached for the cup, half drained it, and went back to eat what was left. When the platter was empty, he drank what was left in the cup, placed silver beside the plate, and arose. He looked one last time at the dawdling stranger. This time their eyes met, held for a moment, then drifted apart.

Lockwood went out under the overhang, turned up his collar, and watched a light spring wagon slewing its way toward the general store. He waited. When the stranger came out, he reset his hat before peering both ways. He saw Lockwood as he spoke to him. "Are you lookin' for someone, mister?"

The younger man's gaze was stone steady. He considered Lockwood while sucking his teeth. He made no attempt to reply as he turned and strode north in the direction of the general store, beyond that the abstract office, and eventually the saloon.

Stuart appeared in the cafe doorway, drying his hands on a soiled apron. He peered northward where the man with the black hat was turning in up at the general store. When the man passed from sight, the cafe man faced Lockwood. "If things was normal, I'd say he's just some close-mouthed drifter. But things ain't normal, not with him ridin' in from the cottonwood camp."

Lockwood went down to the livery barn to look in on his horse. The animal was standing hip-shot, eyes almost closed, enjoying the aftermath of a big bait of timothy hay. The livery man approached wearing a threadbare old blanket coat with a cud in his cheek. He leaned on the stall door also looking at the dozing animal.

Lockwood had a question. "This kind of weather you don't do much business?"

The large-bearded man continued to lean, studying Lockwood's horse when he replied. "The hell of this business is that when the weather's bad, folks don't go out much . . . but horses go right on eating." He faced around. "I was a blacksmith for fifteen years, then I give it up because some mornings I could hardly get out of bed. You want to know about the feller from the freighter camp?" At Lockwood's expression of surprise the big man grinned. "He come in up at the cafe while I was eating. Stuart told me where he'd seen him ride in from. Come along, his horse is down near the alley on the north side."

The animal was a sturdy seal brown with a good eye, nice head, and no brand. The livery man jutted his jaw. "New shoes all around. It wasn't done across the road. I know local shoein' when I see it."

They went up to the harness room which smelled strongly of stale horse sweat every time it rained. The livery man had a lamp lighted but, since he hadn't cleaned the mantle in weeks, it gave off only half the light it should have.

"There," the livery man said, jutting his jaw. "I don't recognize the maker's name, but it's a pretty well worn saddle."

There were no saddlebags which was a disappointment to Lockwood. Nor was there a saddle boot with the customary Winchester in it. The saddle was old but solid and kept well oiled.

When they turned to leave, the livery man was ahead. As he passed the doorless opening, he nearly collided with the stranger whose black hat was now soggy. The livery man reacted fast for a large man. He bumped the younger man hard, then grabbed the stranger's right arm, and gripped it. The man's fingers were inches from the saw-handle stock of his six-gun.

The livery man made a wolfish smile as he apologized for bumping into the younger man but did not loosen the grip which immobilized the stranger's right arm. As the younger man strained to free his gun arm, the blacksmith spun him around as though he had been a child, gripped the six-gun, and muscled it free. He handed the gun to Lockwood, gripped the stranger up high by his shirt, and propelled him into the harness room.

When the big man released the stranger, the man turned, showing an expressionless face as he said: "What the hell's wrong with you? I come down to get my horse. . . ."

"And shoot someone in the back," the livery man growled. He pointed to the only chair in the room. "Set!"

The stranger sat. He still showed nothing, neither indignation nor anger. The livery man got a fresh cud in his cheek while eyeing the stranger. Lockwood asked where the man had come from and both men who knew otherwise heard the first lie from the stranger.

"Over west of Derby. I been lookin' for work. Anythin' wrong with that?"

Lockwood leaned on the stranger's saddle. The livery man chewed slowly for a moment, turned, and spat out into the runway. When he faced forward again, he said, "Mister you're a damned liar. You come from that freighter camp east a ways."

This time Lockwood thought he caught a glimpse of expression — surprise. He examined the stranger's weapon, wordlessly handed it to the livery man. On the back strap of the handle were six little inlaid silver crosses. The livery man balanced the weapon and handed it back to Lockwood. "Some gunsmith worked it over. It rides in a man's hand with perfect balance. Try the trigger, Mister Lockwood."

First the weapon was unloaded, then Lockwood cocked and dry fired it. His slightest tug caused the hammer to drop. He shook his head at the stranger. "All you got to do is cock that thing and breathe on it. It didn't come that way, mister. I watched you at the cafe. When I was outside and you came out . . . lose your nerve, did you?"

The impassive face remained that way.

The livery man considered the stranger with an expression of disgust. "There's room in the cell for both of them. On your feet."

Whether Bertha thought so or not, the livery man was a savvy individual. He led the way up the back alley to the jailhouse, entered from out back, punched the cold-faced stranger to a bench, and took down a copper ring of keys as Lockwood opened the cell room door.

They were both interested in what would happen when the caged freighter saw the new prisoner, but nothing happened. The man who owned the killer gun only glanced in at the freighter and he, for his part, showed nothing but curiosity as he watched the stranger get locked into a cell.

Back in the dusty office, Lockwood shook his head. "They don't know each other."

The livery man was hanging the key ring back on its peg as he replied, "But they will by morning. I'll tell you what I think, Mister Lockwood. That feller with the customized gun come to kill you."

Lockwood shrugged. "He came to kill someone."

"You," insisted the big-bearded man. "They don't like none of the rest of us or our town, but you played hell with their friends and for that they'll want your hair." As they returned to the alley, the bearded man added, "Come evenin', when I'm through with the chores, I'm goin' to mosey back up here an' convince that new one he'd ought to cooperate with us folks in town."

They parted in the livery barn runway, Lockwood for the long walk from the lower end of Derby to the upper end. Bertha was in her rocker knitting as though there was to be no tomorrow, but this time she didn't let him sit down. She said: "Lady Barlow came by while you was gone. She told me her foreman quit yesterday evening. She asked if I thought you could put up with ridin' and doin' light work now."

"And you told her I couldn't, not yet."

"I told her you could but only real light work, no horse shoein' or anything like that."

Bertha got busy with her needles again.

Lockwood sat down, pushed his legs out, and gazed southward. He had something to consider that made the flat-chested, iron-willed stockwoman lie in far abeyance until Bertha spoke again, this time furiously knitting and refusing to look at Lockwood.

"She said she'd be in tomorrow morning. She has some work to do at the bank, then she'll come by, and the pair of you can ride out to the ranch."

Lockwood stared at the older woman. "Have you forgot all that talk about savin' the town, an' all?"

"No, I haven't forgotten a single damned word I said to you, but then you also said there was enough men in town to take care of things . . . an' you'll be ten miles away."

He sat gazing at her. His knowledge of women was not extensive to start with, and with women like Bertha Bradley he'd had no experience at all.

Chapter Six

IN THE EYE OF THE STORM

The rain alternated between deluge and drizzle and kept up for the next two days. If that wasn't bad enough, there was intermittent wind rattling roof shingles from the north, then from the east. Things in Derby drew down to minimum exposure for man and beast. Lady Barlow didn't appear, nor did Bertha expect her to in the rain.

Billy Phelps's pool hall did a good business as did Andrew Lipton's water hole. He had the big iron stove fired up, less because of the roof-rattling wind than because of the creeping, all-pervading dampness.

Lockwood's leg dully ached. Bertha nodded sagely about that. "For as long as you live," she stated, "you'll be able to guess the comin' weather like old men do." She smiled.

Lockwood went down to the jailhouse. His progress was abetted where there were overhangs in front of stores, but he still got about half soaked before he pushed open the door and was met by a heavy wave of heat. Abel

Starr, the big hairy-faced livery man, was seated on a cocked-back chair, whittling. He snapped the knife shut as Lockwood closed the door. Across the room the little iron stove was popping. With each pop, smoke sprang from around the stove's door and from the single large round lid on the top. The office smelled of pine wood.

The livery man had placed a scarred old coffee pot on the lid but only recently. The coffee was not yet boiling. Outside the wind-driven rain beat unmercifully against the single, recessed little barred window in the roadway wall. The livery man shook his head. All it would take to devastate his protective shelter would be for that damned wind to hurl a stick against the glass.

Lockwood stood by the stove, watching Abel whose nerves were edgy like every other set of nerves in town — for the time being not about impending freighter trouble but because of the storm.

The jailhouse had been built from large fir logs with adequate chinking between so, while the storm was audible, it was a lot less so than in other structures around town. Lockwood didn't have to raise his voice when he said, "How're the prisoners?"

Abel didn't answer. He looked at Lockwood, arose, opened the cell-room door, and jerked his head. He did not follow Lockwood inside. He remained by the door with a bleak expression.

When Lockwood returned, the livery man shrugged, turned his back to cross over to his chair, before facing around as he sat.

Lockwood said: "Did it work?"

The livery man inclined his head. "Like a physic. I was right. He come here to kill you. For a hunnert dollars."

Lockwood went to a wall bench and eased down as a particularly fierce wind gust scrabbled along the eaves seeking a way inside.

"His name's Denton Middleton. He's twenty-four years old. He come from Texas, but the last few years he's been doin' his chores between Montana an' down here." Abel shoved out oaken legs. "He was a shirt-tail relative to the Hanson boys. A freighter by the name of Halloran run him down, told him what you'd done. Halloran come onto him at a place called Dunston. I never heard of it."

Lockwood quietly said, "I have."

"That other one's name is Pete Whipple. He yelled and cussed while I convinced Middleton he'd ought to tell me what I wanted to know. When I was finished, I went over to his cell. That scrawny yellow dog cringed in the back, swearin' he'd tell me whatever

I wanted to know if I just kept out of his cell." The big man paused to resettle in the chair and eye the pot on the stove which was beginning to boil. "The head Injun out there is Walter Fromm. I know him. He's been haulin' freight for years. I never liked him. He's a loud-mouthed Missourian. Whatever someone else has done, he's done it bigger an' better."

Abel arose to remove the pot from the stove and fill two tin cups. He took one to Lockwood and returned to the chair with the other one. It was too hot to drink so he put the cup aside. Lockwood did the same, not only because it was too hot but also because it looked and smelled like black death.

Someone was beating on the door from the outside. The livery man arose to open it, and along with the tan-hided cafe man a wild gust of wind-driven rain came in. He went to stand by the stove and catch his breath. The road was a quagmire. It had taken all his breath and muscle to get across to the jailhouse.

Lockwood offered him his tin cup, which the cafe man took and half emptied, hot or not. As he put the cup aside, he said: "Walt Fromm's up at the saloon with six armed freighters. They want to know what become of a couple of friends of theirs."

The livery man replied gruffly. "They're dry an' been fed. Fromm can come see 'em any time he wants to. I'll bust half his ribs an' lock him up too."

Stuart Bentley went to share the bench where Lockwood was sitting. "They're loaded for bear."

"How many?"

"Seven, countin' Walt Fromm."

The livery man did not look worried. "You want to go around an' let the vigilantes know? Seven ain't enough, Stuart. Fromm needs twice that many."

The cafe man knew about warring against odds. This time he liked the notion that the odds would be on the other side. As he arose, another massive gust of wind struck the unmovable log jailhouse. Stuart shook his head. "I'd look more kindly on it if them damned fools'd held off until this storm has passed."

Again a furious blast of chilly, wet air entered as the cafe man opened and closed the door.

Lockwood went to stand by the little recessed, barred window. All he could make out were distorted outlines of buildings on the east side of the road. Some hapless soul moved in an awkward, hunched run across the way, his silhouette distorted by the rain-streaked pane of glass.

Abel Starr went to stand by the stove after he refilled his tin cup. He made a disgruntled comment about the weather. "At least nothing'll burn. That's what worried most folks. Them freighters ain't above burnin' a town."

Lockwood saw that distorted, hunched figure bucking wind on his way in the direction of the general store from wherever he had been. He told himself it was too late for springtime torrents. At least in places where he'd been. He stood squinting but did not see any movement. Even the hunched figure was no longer in sight.

Miles south was New Mexico where it didn't snow, at least not if a man rode far enough from the upland border of Colorado. He should have asked around about rain. He'd bucked his share of wind, and he'd slogged through his share of mud, usually with ice crystals in it. He had never liked wind but, where he had spent years working ranges, they rarely arrived at the same time. Not like this, anyway.

The livery man spoke from back by the stove. "Mister Lockwood, did it ever come to you there's got to be an easier way to serve the Lord than tryin' to make a livin' in this kind of country?"

Lockwood turned and nodded. "Somethin' else come to me, Mister Starr. It's nothin' I like, but if it worked, it'd settle things."

The bearded man barely inclined his head. "I'm listening."

"You won't like it."

"I'm still listenin', Mister Lockwood."

"How far is that freighter camp from town?"

"Mile an' a half. No more'n two miles."

Lockwood sighed, set his back to the window, and spoke. "There's seven in town includin' their head In'ian. How many would you guess are still out there?"

This time the livery man filled a tin cup with coffee and stood with heat on his backsides as he gazed at Lockwood. Eventually he dryly said: "You're right, I won't like it. Neither will any of the vigilantes."

Lockwood sat in the chair the livery man had vacated. "It'll be better than waitin' for dry weather . . . when buildings are dry."

"An' what about those men up at the saloon?"

"Lock 'em up with their friends."

Abel Starr gazed steadily at the seated man. "Just how do we go about doin' that? Stuart said they're armed to the teeth and they'll be spoilin' for a fight. It'll take time to get the vigilantes ready."

Lockwood's gaze remained on the man by the stove, holding his tin cup, making no move to raise it. "Two choices," he told the livery man. "Go out yonder where they'll be tryin' to stay dry an' warm, use the storm to conceal us as best we can, run their horses an' mules out of the country, fight 'em if we can't avoid it, an' slip back to town."

"What's the other choice, Mister Lockwood?"

"Brace the men at the saloon. If there's a way in from the alley, get as much of an edge as possible. Fight if we got to."

Abel went over to the bench near the empty gun rack on the west wall, sat down, and finally tasted his coffee. He shook his head, emptied the cup, settled back, gazing across the room. "I wouldn't bet how many townsmen'll like your idea. It's bad out there. We'll be plowin' through mud up to our hocks."

Lockwood nodded in agreement. "They can stay inside near the stove an' do nothin', Mister Starr. That's fine with me. I was just passin' through. I got no interest in a single one of their buildings."

The livery man sat listening to the raging storm, his chin sunk on his chest, and studied his boots for a long time before speaking again. What troubled him most was not walking out there, although that held no appeal and he had to admit the freighter camp would have its inhabitants out of the storm, and also the notion that armed men might sneak up on the camp would not occur to the men out there and, if it did, the limited visibility, powerful wind, and stinging rain would conceal stalkers and any noise they might make. No, what troubled him most was leaving the armed, belligerent freighters in town while he and others would be stalking their camp. Even that might not be critical but, if there was one gunshot out there, the wind could carry the sound to town. He frowned at Lockwood.

"It's the ones in town that worry me. I don't like havin' them behind us after we take the vigilantes out yonder. That'd be leavin' the town with damned poor protection."

Lockwood rolled and lighted a smoke. He did not intend to argue. He still felt more detached from Derby's troubles than responsible for them.

This time, when a visitor arrived, he did not knock. He punched the door open, slammed it, waited for the little stove's smoke gusts to dissipate, then spoke to the livery man acting as though Lockwood was not there.

"Stuart sent me to tell you more of 'em come. Now there's about thirteen of 'em an' they're loadin' up on Dutch courage."

The livery man's gaze drifted to Lockwood. "I guess one of them choices has been made for us."

The messenger, who was powerfully built with brownish blond hair, went to the stove to stand with his back to it. Lockwood did not know him, but he knew who he was, the blacksmith's helper, the man who had joined Bertha getting Lockwood up to the rooming house after the fight at the cafe.

Abel said: "That's a gawdamned army, Mister Lockwood."

There was no longer any question of leaving town, but if there had been, about all that could have been accomplished at the cottonwood camp was stampede the horses. Right now stampeding horses, like Lady Barlow, was not important.

Lockwood asked the powerfully-built blond man if he was aware whether or not the vigilantes knew what had happened. The blacksmith's helper grimaced. "The noise they're makin' at the saloon . . . even the storm ain't enough to muffle it. I'd say everyone in town knows."

Lockwood returned his attention to the livery man. "The vigilantes," he said.

Abel Starr nodded. He asked the blacksmith's helper if he could maybe find Stuart and the pair of them tell the townsmen to gather over in back of the saloon.

The young man agreed by nodding his head. "I don't need Stuart. I can do it myself. But what're they supposed to do? By now I'd guess everyone knows there's goin' to be a fight."

The livery man looked enquiringly at Lockwood. For ten seconds or so the room was quiet before Lockwood spoke again. He wished for the tenth time the Army was closer, but it wasn't, and he was again being turned to for leadership in an affair he had never encountered before, and sat for a moment trying to find an answer.

"First off, are their horses out front of the saloon?"

The younger man nodded.

"They've got to be turned loose."

Both the blacksmith's helper and the livery man nodded and waited for what came next.

"The vigilantes split up, part in doorways opposite the saloon. Hiding places of some kind. The rest go around to the alley behind the saloon."

Again his listeners nodded and waited.

Lockwood looked at them and swore to himself. *This was impossible. It wasn't his*

town. It wasn't his fight, but even if it was. . . .
"We'll yell for them to put down their guns and come out, or we'll come in with shotguns."

The younger man accepted that, but the livery man scowled. "Mister Lockwood, they been drinkin' in there. They don't scare easy even sober, an' there aren't that many shotguns in the whole town."

"You got a better idea, Mister Starr?"

The livery man didn't, but the blacksmith's helper had. "We got a barrel of sulphur at the shop. We use it in brazin' and mixed with other stuff for hammerin' steel together." They looked blankly at the younger man until he finished what he had to say. "If someone was to toss five or six sulphur bundles through the door, lighted like bombs . . . ," he paused to smile. "That stuff smolders to beat hell. Inside a building it'd make 'em blind an' sicker'n dogs. Even at the smithy with everythin' open we got to be careful. A good dose will make a man heave up his boot straps."

The wind howled, the window rattled, streaks of water blocked out visibility inside or out. Lockwood and the livery man looked at each other, then at the blacksmith's helper.

Because he thought they were impressed

with his idea, he said: "I can go down there, make up some of them little bombs. It'll maybe take me fifteen minutes. By that time you fellers can be hid across the road. Maybe you could even round up some of the others."

Lockwood nodded. He and the livery man watched the blacksmith's helper depart wearing the expression of a child who has just made a breathtaking discovery about himself. After the door closed and the stove's gusting dissipated, the livery man dryly remarked, "That's the damndest idea I ever heard of. Will it work?"

Lockwood had no idea whether it would or not, but he was willing to see it tried. "If it'll just smoke some of them out into the open. . . ."

Abel shot to his feet. For a moment he listened to the storm. It seemed to be subsiding, not much but a little. Hell, it had to end sometime.

"We got to find Stuart an' the others. How's your leg?"

Lockwood stood up. It felt fine. Right at this moment, if it had been amputated at the knee, it would have felt fine. The blacksmith's helper had got him out of a dilemma he was satisfied he would never have been able to get out of by himself.

As they stood by the door, the livery man thought of something and scowled. "Suppose it don't work an' they get down here an' free the prisoners?"

Lockwood's reply moved the livery man to grasp the latch and lift. "If it don't work, they can have the damned prisoners. But it will work. You know why?"

"Why?"

"Because it has to. Let's go."

Chapter Seven

A HARROWING NIGHT

Subsiding or not, the storm still could take a man's breath away and reach beneath everything he wore to chill his bones. Stuart's experience crossing the roadway was no different when Lockwood and the livery man crossed it. If anything the mud was deeper and runnels of chocolaty water were swifter.

If either man had risked looking skyward as they felt their way gingerly around boulders and potholes, they would have noticed that the moon was visible. The ghostly light it gave off showed wide rifts in the scudding low clouds. The storm was unraveling westerly ahead of a driving wind.

Once, during a lull, they heard loud male voices from the direction of Lipton's saloon. By the time they got around to the east-side alley men were arriving wrapped in black slickers that shone darkly. Not as many arrived as the livery man would have liked to see, but Lockwood thought there were about eleven of them with an occasional shiny black shadow coming into view. Stuart was wearing someone's slicker which fit well enough except for the sleeves. His arms stuck out four or five inches below the cuffs.

Lockwood explained what they had in mind and, while a number of vigilantes looked pleased, some did not, which Lockwood understood. It was a totally bizarre idea. He hadn't thought it would work either. Right now with rain pelting them he gave it a fifty-fifty chance. He didn't know anything about sulphur bombs.

Someone opened an alley door northward from the saloon. The black silhouettes faded from sight. The man stood looking up for several minutes, finished what he'd come out for, and went back inside. There was an outhouse, but it was across the alley and southward nearly thirty yards. What the man in the doorway did actually did not require an outhouse. Anyway, it was too stormy to trudge thirty yards and back.

Several more men arrived. One was in a new-fangled yellow slicker which turned water admirably but among skulkers in black stood out like a sore thumb.

Abel counted, turned to Lockwood, and said: "Sixteen. We got to wait anyway. There'll be more."

The vigilantes were nervous and uncomfortable. Abel Starr explained the delay and got some wide-eyed looks and several expressions of skepticism and disgust. One man, tall and lanky, scoffed, "In this wind?"

Abel gave a quick, irritable reply. "They'll be flung inside."

"There's wind in there too."

The livery man's annoyance was clear as he said: "Nowhere nearly enough . . . if he makes them bombs right and gets 'em inside . . . an' if they do what he said they'd do."

"If . . . ," grumbled the unidentifiable man whose head and most of his face was hidden inside a cowl-like part of his slicker.

The livery man turned on him. "You know some better way?"

"Sure, slip up to the windows and start shooting."

That suggestion went down with no one, not even others like the lanky man who was spoiling for a fight. The livery man replied dryly. "Sure, there's local men in there too."

The lanky man moved toward the rear of the crowd, muttering to himself. A massively-built man of unexceptional height pushed through the crowd. All Lockwood could see of his face was a beard that seemed even in semi-darkness to have a reddish tinge to it. Lockwood recognized him but couldn't place him. He was Ezra Evans, the town blacksmith. Now, he stood facing the livery man, who was taller but no broader, and asked a question. "You expect them to come out the back door?"

Lockwood replied because the livery man had shown that the longer they stood in the storm waiting the shorter his temper was getting.

"Most of us'll be around front, across the road, and under cover. They'll come out the front door. If they don't, you stay back here and yell if they come out the back. I'd guess they'll run out the same way they come in . . . like livestock that uses trails an' gates they always used."

Someone lighted a smoke inside the cowl of his shiny slicker. For seconds a lean, lantern-jawed face showed clearly before the light died and only a glowing tip was left which reddened as the smoker inhaled and paled-out when he exhaled.

Men stamped their feet, rubbed gloved and mittened hands, occasionally stole a look skyward where the moon was playing hide-and-seek among ragged and wind-driven clouds. The blacksmith's helper arrived from southward holding his slicker so that the little sulphur bombs were kept dry. He had taken so long because he had made six.

Men crowded. The blacksmith examined

one of the little bombs carefully, noted how the thick waxed paper had been twisted so that each bomb had about a six-inch wick, and smiled at his helper. "You're goin' to make your mark someday, Carl."

Abel and another man moved up the south side of the saloon as far as they could go before an adjoining building's overhang stopped them. Lockwood and the cafe man went south to the dog-trot from which the cafe man had shot and killed a freighter, passed up through, emerged into blustery, wet darkness which showed not a single lighted structure within visual distance.

Three men followed. All five came out of the dog-trot soundlessly and more or less unnoticeably until they moved. Stuart had his old horse pistol inside his coat and under his slicker. He could not have reached his weapon without having plenty of time; on the other hand his black powder weapon was particularly liable to misfire if it got wet.

The noise in Lipton's saloon was audible except when the wind blew northward, away from the stalkers. Lockwood guessed the freighters in there were in no hurry to leave a dry place with whiskey and companions to go down and make a break-out attempt for their friends.

Stuart nudged Lockwood. A crouched,

stealthy shadow was alongside the south wall of the saloon making careful progress in the direction of the badly washed roadway until it reached the building's corner and straightened up, seemed to hesitate, was forced to lean into a particular fierce gust of wind which sped toward the five black statues in front of the dog-trot. As it broke against them and hurried on, the cafe man said: "I smelled somethin' burnin'."

Lockwood led the way across the road, which was not only ankle deep in mud but which also had two-foot gullies under the muddy water. It was a particularly bad time. They wanted to get across rapidly, but the footing was too treacherous for haste. Saloon lights shone where they were groping their way. Lockwood looked over his shoulder several times. If they were to be caught in the open, this would be the time.

It was close. An unsteady man lurched past the spindle doors. Wind and stinging rain made him gasp and crouch as he went toward the dog-trot, down into it, and remained there until Lockwood and his companions were on the far duckboards. They had seen him and, pressed flat, were motionless until the man came out of the dog-trot. His return hike was steadier than his out-going hike. Cold and driving rain had cleared some of the cobwebs from his brain, but he was in a hurry, looking neither right nor left and disappearing inside the saloon.

He had scarcely got inside when someone over there with a bull-bass voice roared. Lockwood had lost sight of the man alongside the building. One of his companions grunted and pointed. Lockwood saw a shiny black shape step up to one side of the saloon door and make a hurling motion. He did this five times before shouting, cursing, and sounds of chairs being upended drove him away.

Lockwood and his companions had a dingy store front at their backs and a leaky wooden overhang above. While they were motionless, it would have been hard to make them out even without the storm. They became part of it.

The black, shiny shadow reappeared to hurl his last sulphur bomb, was preparing to step in front of the door to make his cast when a coughing, staggering man came out. The violently swinging door on the north side struck the shadow. He hurled his projectile even as he fought for balance.

The man who had burst forth leaned to cough violently. He had no inkling how close the shadow was. Lockwood saw the pistol rise and fall. The retching man went head first off the duckboards into the mud. He rolled, made an awkward, instinctive attempt to arise, fell back, and crawled to the plank walk where he collapsed. The shadow disappeared northward.

A man close by said: "One down."

No one commented. Every eye was on the spindle doors. Men in the saloon were cursing, yelling, coughing, bumping tables, bumping each other, falling, and retching.

Lockwood said: "Let's go," and started back across the road. The sulphur bombs had done better than he had expected, mainly because there had been six of them and, unbeknownst to the men outside, men gagging from smoke had tried to kick the burning small objects. The result was not at all what they expected; sulphur, once ignited, did not stop smoldering easily.

The smell reached where five black shapes were recrossing, only this time directly toward the front of the saloon. All but one of them had a six-gun gripped at his side as he floundered his way back the way he had come.

Stuart Bentley pushed ahead without watching his footing. He was concentrating on the saloon's doorway, but no one emerged, and the cafe man stepped where there was a hole, wind milled for balance, and fell.

Lockwood was close enough to grab cloth and help Bentley recover, but his old pistol was now useless. When they reached the far plank walk, the cafe man went over where the muddy, soggy individual was lying who had been hit over the head, took the man's side arm, which was not only fully loaded but was a much later and vastly improved model of his own weapon. He paused to dry both hands on the downed man's shirt then turned.

Lockwood did not rush inside. He stood off to one side and peeked in. As he did this, a rush of inside air reached him. The sulphur scent was almost overwhelming, but the moment it was outside the building the wind seized it, shredded it, and bore it swiftly away.

He had glimpsed men through smoke. None was still but neither did they appear to have direction. One man stumbled almost to the door before he fell, and another man fell over him. Behind his bar Andrew Lipton was holding a wet cloth over his lower face. His eyes stung and watered which Lockwood could not see.

The smoke was everywhere, even the far corners of the saloon, and it was a large room. It was dense with smoldering balls of sulphur continually adding to the limited visibility.

Several men joined Lockwood's party and one, the blacksmith's helper, grinned from ear to ear. Lockwood took a leaf from the saloonman's book. He held his bandanna out for the rain to soak it, held it across his face with his left hand, and entered the saloon. His companions followed, also holding up bandannas.

Lockwood knew none of the freighters. He grabbed the first one he encountered, flung him toward the door, and sought another one. It did not take long to empty the saloon. Lockwood and his companions had the best of all reasons to make their gather quickly. Eyes watered copiously if exposed long to sulphur fumes.

They emptied the saloon by which time all the vigilantes had joined them out front. Only Andrew Lipton was left in his saloon. He had watched the capture of his customers with tears flowing. He certainly recognized Lockwood. He probably recognized individual vigilantes too, but he remained behind his bar like part of the woodwork.

Fresh air helped but not immediately. Lockwood had his hands full trying to herd half-drunk, badly gassed freighters across the roadway. Two of his prisoners dropped completely from sight only to pop up swearing, gagging, and spitting out muddy water.

The jailhouse office was crowded. Mud dripped. Shaking men crowded around the stove which had to be stoked to life. When Abel, the livery man, met Lockwood, he rolled his eyes as though to imply he had not believed the idea of sulphur bombs was practical.

The difficulty once everyone was inside out of the storm was to get names. Several freighters were very ill. Others could give names but only amid fits of coughing and the drying of watering eyes.

The office smelled of burnt sulphur. Stuart Bentley and another man went among the freighters collecting weapons. The livery man stood aside. He knew several of the freighters by sight, as did most folks in Derby. They were the men who had been hauling into town for years. The livery man and the blacksmith remained aloof, watching, occasionally commenting, satisfied that the far-fetched notion of the blacksmith's helper had culminated satisfactorily.

Stuart found a hide-out weapon. Another vigilante found a wicked-bladed double-edge Arkansas toothpick in a boot upper. After that they went over the freighters roughly and thoroughly.

A dark-eyed, blunt-jawed man badly in need of shearing came over to Lockwood, mopped his eyes, and said: "Who's the law here?"

Before Lockwood could reply, Stuart Bentley jerked a thumb in Lockwood's direction and said: "He is."

The swarthy man lowered his bandanna as he said, "I'm Walt Fromm. Where's your badge?"

Lockwood smiled at the swarthy man without humor, raised his six-gun, cocked it, and kept smiling as he said, "In my hand."

The freighter was surprised but not intimidated. "You'll be Cuff Lockwood."

"Yep. An' you're boss of the freighters."

"Not boss. We got no boss. I'm just a freighter like the rest of 'em. Mister Lockwood, unless you're a legal town marshal an' unless you get a legal writ to show why we're being held, you got no call to keep us."

Lockwood's mirthless smile faded. He went after the copper key ring, took it to the cell-room door with him, opened the door, and jerked his head. "You first, Mister Fromm."

A strapping large man built like a gorilla said, "Like hell. If there's no legal lawman, there ain't no legal arrests. You boys ready to go?"

They undoubtedly were not only ready to leave the jailhouse but eager to do so. They looked at the vigilantes, at Lockwood, and finally at Walt Fromm. Not a one of them moved toward the door.

The big freighter swore. "What'n hell's wrong with you? Up at the saloon you had considerable to say about Derby an' its folks . . . all the things you was goin' to do to 'em. Now you're standin' there like a herd of sick snakes."

Abel Starr moved slowly forward, took the big man's measure, and hit him. The freighter crumpled without a sound. The livery man faced the other prisoners. "Any of you gents want to take it up where your friend left off?"

Evidently no one was willing, not with that ham-handed livery man staring at them.

A freighter, rehanging the *olla* after drinking from it, spoke without completely facing around. "I told you. I told you ten times over . . . this wasn't the way to do it. Well, you liked Walt's idea over mine, now look where we are."

Fromm snarled at the freighter. "You're a danged disgrace. Who was it out yonder called for firin' the place an' shootin' folks by firelight?"

The out-spoken man gave stare for stare with Fromm. "If you're trying to make out that was my idea, there's men in this room who'll swear about whose idea that was, Walt . . . yours!"

Lockwood said: *"Shut up!"* He pointed down into the cell room. *"Move!"*

They moved. Lockwood went ahead to open steel doors. He told which men to enter each cell. When they were locked in, he let go a big rattling sigh, went back up front, kicked the door closed, flung the copper ring of keys on the old dusty desk, and gazed around. For as long as no one spoke, the only sound was of the storm. It was lessening in its fury, the slashing rain now a steady downpour, the wind becoming intermittent.

Someone put the coffee pot atop the stove. Before it boiled, most of the townsmen had departed. With more room the remaining vigilantes found places to sit. Some went to work rolling smokes. The blacksmith gave way on a bench for his helper.

The cafe man mightily yawned as he said, "I got to fire up for the breakfast trade. Anyone want to go up yonder and drag that feller who got hit over the head down here?"

No one moved. The cafe man shrugged and departed.

The livery man thought about the horses their prisoners had ridden into town, said he'd go find them, take them down to his barn, and see they were fed in a dry place.

After he left, the blacksmith ran bent fingers through his hair and leaned back, gazing at the stove as he said, "What'll we do with 'em, an' what about the ones out at their cottonwood camp?"

No one replied. It was late. Every man was tired. Most were also wet. All of them had been chilled. They had also come close to exhausting their reserves of energy. It was hot in the office and getting hotter. Lockwood's leg ached, probably from crossing and recrossing the muddy road. He was willing to let things wait until tomorrow and said so. He was the last to leave the jailhouse. No one had drunk the coffee. He set the damper, blew out the lamp, took the key ring with him, locked the jailhouse from the outside, and headed for the rooming house. When he was passing the saloon on the opposite side of the road, he noticed that it was dark.

But there was one light burning. When he stopped to kick mud off his boots, the noise brought Bertha to the door. She was swaddled in an old cotton bathrobe and was holding a candle. She held the door for Lockwood then padded along behind him to his room and stood in the doorway.

He shed his hat, draped his shell belt and holstered Colt over the back of a chair, sank down on the edge of the bed, and looked at her. "They're locked up."

"All of them?"

"All but one who got hit over the head. I don't know what became of him but, when I passed the saloon, he was no longer lying out front. I guess he went back to their camp."

"I didn't hear gunfire."

"There wasn't any. There's some sick fellers in the cells. Otherwise there was the feller who got hit on the head."

"How did you do it?"

"*I* didn't do it, Bertha. The blacksmith's helper made some little bombs full of sulphur. He pitched 'em into the saloon. The rest of it was easy enough. They breathed enough of that smoke so's they couldn't find their behinds with both hands."

"No one was hurt? I mean, none of the men from town?"

"No."

Lockwood hoisted one foot after the other and shed his boots. He stood up to shuck out of his shirt. Bertha did not take the hint. "How is your leg?"

"It aches from walkin' through mud dang near to my hocks in the road."

"I better look at it. The bandage is bound to need changin'."

Lockwood sighed. "In the morning, Bertha. Right now I could sleep the clock around. Good night."

She did not leave immediately. She stood gazing at him until candle wax fell on her knuckles, then she swore and closed the door after herself.

Lockwood stood a moment looking at the door, wondering if she had fretted over her late husband as she was doing over him.

She had.

Chapter Eight

SUNSHINE FOR A CHANGE

When Lockwood awakened, there was sunlight everywhere. Even his room was dazzlingly bright. By the time he got back from cleaning up out back, the ground was steaming.

He went down to the cafe, where men were talking more than eating with the cafe man neglecting his duties as he took part in the talk. When Lockwood entered, the conversation dwindled but did not stop. The cafe man came over. Before Lockwood could give his order, the cafe man said: "Ezra just left. Them fellers at the jailhouse is raisin' Cain."

Lockwood nodded, asked for breakfast and, when the cafe man did not move, he also said: "I expect they got to be fed."

That brought a surly response from a customer. "Let 'em starve. I dang near got the grippe last night from gettin' soaked."

Another diner also had a comment to make. "We looked high 'n' low for that one Carl hit over the head. Most likely he got back to their camp. I don't like the idea of one of them bein' loose."

Lockwood was hungry. The cafe man got him coffee then asked a question which was in everyone else's mind. "What'll we do with 'em? The circuit ridin' judge ain't due for another month."

Lockwood's hunger was only slightly abated by coffee. He regarded the cafe man steadily as he said, "I'd take it kindly if you'd get my breakfast, Stuart."

The cafe man scuttled toward his kitchen as a heavily whiskered diner said, "Hang 'em, for all I care."

Someone laughed. "Ain't that much rope in town, Eli." This same man turned his attention to Lockwood. "We could hold a kangaroo court. I, for one, don't much like the notion of feedin' that many prisoners out of town funds."

Before Lockwood could speak, another townsman said: "Good idea. Sam'll hold court up at the fire house like the circuit rider does."

The cafe man brought Lockwood's breakfast who took no further part in the talk, did not even make an effort to listen. He concentrated on eating.

Eventually, as the diners thinned out, the cafe man got himself a cup of Java, leaned on his pie table opposite Lockwood, and reminisced. "You believe in omens, Mister Lockwood?"

The process of swallowing inhibited an immediate answer so Lockwood shook his head.

The cafe man was undaunted. "Sun come out. I see that as an omen. All we got to do now is punish those bastards an' things'll get back to normal."

Lockwood nodded, chewed, swallowed, and reached for his coffee. He felt better on a full stomach. He even smiled at the cafe man. "It's your town," he said.

The cafe man interpreted that correctly. "You're leavin'?"

"As soon as I pay Bertha and saddle up."

The cafe man regarded Lockwood for a moment before speaking again. "Well, can't say as I blame you. It's good ridin' weather. You got a destination in mind?"

"Any place it don't snow. South into New Mexico I expect."

"It snows there. Not 'way down on the desert, but it's hell tryin' to make a livin' that far south. Years back I rode down there. Nice country up north, over the line from Colorado, but it snows there. You'll have to go a fair distance southward. I never liked that desert country."

"I never liked snow to my crotch," Lockwood responded and arose to count out silver for his meal.

Outside, roadway mud was caking on top; otherwise it was like gumbo, as Lockwood went south to the livery barn where the bearded, large, tobacco-chewing proprietor was out back, leaning on a corral across the alley doing two things of which he was particularly fond: chewing a fresh cud of molasses-cured and listening to horses eat. He nodded when Lockwood came up, spat, and said, "Sun feels mighty good on a man's back," then, before Lockwood had a chance to reply, he also said, "Folks are frettin' about havin' a jail full of freighters."

Lockwood told him about the idea of holding a kangaroo court. The livery man brightened. "All right. We could fine each of 'em maybe as much as ten dollars, and give 'em a choice of never returning or gettin' hung if they do."

Lockwood shrugged. Whatever Derby did with the troublesome freighters was up to the town. He and the livery man went back inside, up the runway to the stall containing Lockwood's animal. When they stopped there, the livery man jettisoned his cud, frowned slightly as he gazed at his companion, and waited for Lockwood to say it.

"If you'll cuff him an' maybe pour half a can of rolled barley into his manger, I'll be back directly after I settle up with Bertha."

The livery man nodded, said nothing, and watched Lockwood go back up out into the roadway sunshine. He'd had what he considered a really scintillating idea when he had awakened this morning. Get the town council to hire Lockwood as town marshal.

People were abroad, mostly staying on plank walks unless absolute necessity required them to cross through mud to the opposite sidewalk. Lockwood was greeted and smiled at by people he did not know and for the most part had never seen before. He was passing the corral yard about four or five hundred feet from the rooming house when a man called from a doorway. The man was a turkey-necked, rawboned individual who owned the local harness works.

Lockwood remembered him from last night. He had been the grumbling dissenter in the poncho whose hood nearly concealed the man's face. As Lockwood twisted to return the saddler's wave, a gunshot sounded from across the roadway, loud enough to rattle windows and to turn the harness maker rigid in his doorway.

Lockwood felt pain this time. It spiraled up through him like fire. As he went down, someone over in front of Lipton's saloon squawked like a wild turkey. Lockwood never lost consciousness. He could feel blood gushing when he tried to roll into a sitting position.

The turkey-necked older man with a beeswax-stiffened apron got untracked and ran forward. There was one virtue shared by all frontiersmen of his kind — they knew how to stop bleeding. But it required work and straining. The old man's arms were bloody to the elbow before others arrived to gawk and swivel in the direction of the dog-trot from where the shot had come.

He got most of the bleeding stopped by tearing Lockwood's shirt to stuff in the wound. The cafe man came in a high lope from across the road southward. Andrew Lipton also ran over, for once without his barman's apron.

The person who arrived last and who took charge was Bertha. She had a companion, that rawboned, flat-chested, steely-eyed *ranchera* named Lady Barlow. Between them they snarled for men to carry the gun-shot victim to his room up the road northward.

Lady Barlow did not enter the rooming house. She went back across the road and down to the general store where one of her riders was helping load the supply wagon.

She sent the rider to search for the ambusher, and her last words were: "If you find the son of a bitch, shoot him."

By the time she got up to the rooming house, the hallway was full of milling people. Even Lockwood's room was full of watchers as Bertha worked over the man on the bed whose bleeding was soaking her flannel sheet and the blankets.

Lady Barlow was experienced in one thing — taking charge. She thinned out the hallway crowd, got into the room, and snarled for more onlookers to "get the hell out and stay out!"

The old harness maker returned from cleaning up out back, holding a flat pony of whiskey for the patient. Bertha fixed him with her fierce glare, took the bottle, upended it, swallowed twice, handed the bottle back, and said, "He don't need this. Go down to the store and fetch back some laudanum. *Go, dammit! Move.*"

The old man left. Bertha's arms were bloody to the elbow; her shirt-front was also speckled. She had pink hot water in an old basin which got steadily darker red as she worked. When she and Lady Barlow were the only people left, Bertha turned and used a streaked elbow to push back hanging hair as she said: "He bled like a stuck hawg."

"Did you get it stopped?"

"Most of it, yes. I'll stop the rest of it directly. Lady, there's some clean dish towels in a kitchen drawer. Bring all of them."

The rawboned woman leaned to look at the man on the bed whose eyes were closed and whose color was more gray than ruddy. Her gaze drifted to the torn flesh which was already beginning to discolor and swell. She left the room with a long stride.

Bertha saw Lockwood's eyes open. "There's medicine comin'. Just loosen up. I know it hurts. A wound like that'll hurt more than one almost any place else. Did you see him?"

Lockwood spoke a trifle dully. "I didn't see no one. I heard a shot. It came from across the road. I was turnin' to talk to the harness maker."

Bertha nodded. "Damned good thing, Mister Lockwood, otherwise the slug would have broke your spine an' gone through your guts."

A gorilla-like figure filled the doorway. Bertha turned. "There's nothin' you can do, Abel, except get in the way. Unless you want to go find out what's takin' that damned old goat who makes harness so long. I sent him to the store."

The livery man turned, almost bumped

into Lady Barlow, who glared. He sidestepped and kept on going.

Lockwood was beginning to feel more numbness than pain. Right now he would have appreciated that bottle the harness maker had brought. He watched Bertha rinsing her hands and arms, considered the water, and said: "If folks don't quit pickin' on me, I won't have nothin' left to bleed out."

Lady Barlow made a pragmatic remark. "By the time you recover this time, Mister Lockwood, there'll be snow on the ground up to your belt buckle."

He gazed at the angular, thin-lipped woman, said nothing, and closed his eyes. He hadn't mentioned to her his destination. Derby's moccasin telegraph was as swift as the other kind.

The harness maker returned. Bertha took the small bottle to her kitchen. When she returned, the two women propped Lockwood up so he could swallow.

Within ten minutes he was asleep. Bertha continued to hover. Lady Barlow went to make coffee. She brought back two cups. Bertha sipped; her eyes popped wide. There was enough whiskey in the coffee to drown a cat.

The old man hovered under the cold stare

of the female rancher until it made him uncomfortable, then left. He made a bee-line for Lipton's saloon where the only topic under discussion was the shooting.

A number of possibilities was discussed. They boiled down to the bushwhacker's firing from the dog-trot. As for his identity the customers were unanimously of the opinion that it had been a freighter. Speculation centered on the man the blacksmith's helper had knocked unconscious out front of the saloon. All the others were locked up.

Stuart Bentley, the cafe man, wanted to go out to the cottonwood camp, find the gunman, and hang him from the upraised tongue of his own wagon. There was very little dissent until Lady Barlow walked in about an hour later. She told them her rider had gone out there. There was no one around, but one wagon was gone.

She did not elaborate. She did not have to. The cafe man took it up with a suggestion they get a-horseback, overtake the freighter, and either hang him on the spot or bring him back to be locked up with his friends.

Lady Barlow said, if they caught him, they should bring him back. There was in her opinion a possibility the ambusher might not have been the freighter. That idea coming from a person — female or not — whose judgment even confirmed woman-haters had not been able to fault over the years caused some hesitation. Not until late afternoon did the cafe man round up several friends and leave town to find the missing freighter.

Lockwood slept like the dead with Bertha alternating between her other chores and hovering at his bedside. When Lady Barlow came in, she told Bertha she had sent for a physician. She also said she doubted a doctor could do any more for Lockwood than Bertha had done.

They left Lockwood alone, went to Bertha's kitchen, had another cup of laced coffee, and Bertha discovered that Lady Barlow had a pony of whiskey in a pocket of her riding skirt which resolved the mystery of where the liquor had come from earlier with which Lady Barlow had laced their cups of coffee.

Bertha sat slumped, drained to the bone. Even the Irish coffee only marginally improved her dragged-out feeling. She told Lady Barlow that if she was a superstitious person she would believe fate — something anyway — was not going to allow Lockwood to reach New Mexico. Not for a long time anyway. She had no inkling how right she was. If she'd had such an inkling, there would have been an excellent reason for Bertha to believe as the old harness maker believed — in superstitions.

Lady Barlow said something that startled Bertha. "It's too hard on you. Besides you've got the rooming house to run. I'll send a wagon for him in the morning. Between me 'n' my housekeeper we can take turns lookin' out for him and, when the doctor arrives, he can supervise. It'd be best for him, Bertha. 'Round the clock care an' a doctor. It'd let you get your life back to normal. It'd be best for you too."

There were several reasons why Bertha Bradley and Lady Barlow got along so well. One reason was their shared widowhood. Another reason was because both were knowledgeable about men and were therefore both skeptical of them and suspicious of their motives.

With Lady Barlow, who was not as philosophical as Bertha was, it went deeper. Since the passing of her husband, she had come face to face with the condescending attitude of men and, given her iron-hard disposition, her tongue-lashing ability, and her success in areas where women west of the Missouri River did not except in very rare instances compete successfully with men, there was jealousy. Finally, she appeared more masculine than women were supposed to be.

What kept Bertha silent after Lady Barlow's proposal to care for Lockwood at her ranch was the out-of-character compassion Lady Barlow was demonstrating, and a sneaking suspicion that there was more to the offer than simply a desire to be humane. While Bertha was silent, Lady Barlow refilled their cups with mule-shoe coffee. Bertha had succumbed to the wonderfully relaxing influence of the first cup. The second cupful put her in the unique position of being unable to find her bearings easily. She accompanied Lady Barlow to the front verandah, smiled at her out there, and felt for her rocker, afterward to watch the angular woman whose back was usually ramrod straight head for the saloon. She had never envied the other woman's ability to punch through the spindle doors of Andy Lipton's saloon but had come to have respect for a woman who could enter the town's boar's nest, the exclusive gathering place for men, and make them like it.

Lockwood did not come around until after sundown. The lingering let-down from his ingestion of laudanum eased the reviving pain, but by then it was more of an aching discomfort, unless he moved, in which case the pain came down on him like a ton of bricks, so he did not move. But that left his mind unencumbered. When Bertha appeared in the doorway slightly more dowdy than usual with bright eyes and a sweat-shiny face, Lockwood said he was hungry.

She accepted that without leaving the doorway. Men were always hungry or were fixing to be hungry. Years earlier this tendency in her late husband had made Bertha wonder if men didn't just naturally have worms. She came closer, sank onto the chair, unconsciously reached to brush back a straggle of gray-brown hair, and smiled at him.

"Lady Barlow's sent for a doctor. She's sendin' in a rig tomorrow to take you out to her place. Her an' the housekeeper can take 'round-the-clock care . . . better'n I can do, Mister Lockwood."

He was silent so long she eventually arose and mumbled something about getting supper and departed.

Lockwood remained motionless for a long time, considering the ceiling. His conclusion was that folks were doing their damndest to care for him, which he appreciated. But his judgment of the flat-chested, rawboned cow woman was that, if she had concern for the injured, it had to be a smidgin and not a tad more. Not *this* much.

When Bertha returned with supper, Lockwood was asleep. She pondered awakening him, decided not to because she knew folks that had bled-out much for some reason always afterwards required an inordinate amount of sleep. She put the chair at bedside, placed the tray on it, took the cup of coffee back to the kitchen with her — no one in their right mind enjoyed tepid coffee — and ate. That was something else normal folks did not like — eating alone. This evening Bertha picked at her food. The Irish coffee had worn off. The result was not a headache. It was an almost overpowering need for sleep.

Lockwood slept like the dead. The rooming house was quiet after dusk when Lady Barlow arrived at Lockwood's doorway and stood there watching him. The only sound when she arrived, and later when she departed, was the ring of spur rowels.

She went down to the jailhouse where Billy Phelps was cocked back on a chair. He rocked forward and shot up to his feet when the rawboned woman entered. Her cold stare prompted Billy to point at an ajar door as he spoke.

"They brung him in about an hour back, Miz Barlow. He's in one of the cells." Billy was self-conscious. "No one else'd set guard in here at supper time, so I volunteered."

She looked stonily at Billy. "Where's your gun?"

"Gun? Whatever for?"

"A man who guards a prisoner's supposed to have a gun, Billy."

Phelps reddened. "Well, I got one. It's home in a dresser. Miz Barlow, them fellers couldn't get out of their cells if they had a crow bar."

She sniffed, marched down into the gloomy cell room, and halted where a dejected man sat on a wall bunk. They exchanged looks. The prisoner broke off first and looked elsewhere.

Lady Barlow said: "What's your name?"

"My name's Jethro Hubbard an' I know who you are."

Lady Barlow delayed her next statement. "Why did you shoot him?"

The prisoner was a scrawny, nondescript individual of indeterminate age. He could have been thirty or sixty, and he did not answer. He continued to look at the opposite row of steel bars.

Lady Barlow answered for him. "Because he out-smarted you damned freighters and because you was too yellow to face him. How did they catch you?"

"Come up on my blind side."

Lady Barlow sneered. "You fool. Didn't

you know they'd figure out who shot Lockwood and come after you?"

This time the freighter was stung. He glared at the woman beyond his bars. "Why do you think I pulled out? 'Course I knew they'd come after me."

Her voice was contemptuous when she said, "In a wagon? After you tried to kill a man from ambush? No one but a simpleton would try to escape driving a damned wagon. Even on horseback they'd have caught you. Mister Hubbard, I'm going to see to it they hang you."

After she left, the bushwhacker arose, went to the front of his cell, gripped the bars and yelled, "Billy? When I'm out of here, I'm coming back to skin you alive for lettin' that she-catamount in here."

Phelps was leaning back against the wall again as he yelled back, "You hear what she said? She'll get you hung if it's the last thing she ever does. Jethro, if I was you, I'd start prayin' as hard as I could." Billy thought a moment before also saying, "It never done me no good, but you . . . Jethro, that's the only hope you got left."

During the exchange between Lady Barlow and the bushwhacker, the other prisoners had not said a word. After she left and the freighter had yelled to Billy, the other freighters came to life. One of them said: "Jethro, if they don't hang you, s'help me gawd I will. You know what you done? You got everyone in Derby mad as hornets an' that means they ain't going to see no difference between a bushwhackin' son of a bitch an' the rest of us."

Chapter Nine

POR FAVOR

True to her word the following morning Lady Barlow arrived with a light spring wagon with straw and blankets behind and below the seat. She came on horseback. They tied up out front, and she led her two burly rangemen inside, down the hall to Lockwood's room. Instead of saying good morning or asking how he felt, she said: "You need a shave. All right, boys, real easy with him."

Lockwood had no recollection of seeing either of the men before. One was thick through the shoulders with sunburnt fair hair and long sideburns. He winked and smiled at Lockwood; the other rider was thin-lipped and all business. He little more than glanced at the man in the bed as the pair of them moved forward.

Bertha appeared in the doorway. She flushed red. "I'm not sure you'd ought to do this," she told Lady Barlow. "That's a long haul an' he can't stand to lose much more blood."

The angular woman smiled. It was like

crinkling paper. "There's a bed of straw in the rig and plenty of blankets. We know every pothole." Lady Barlow faced the men. "Real gentle now."

She and Bertha stood aside as the cowboys eased around the doorway so that Lockwood would not be bumped. They went directly down the hall, kicked the door open, and with more room went to the wagon, unchained the tailgate, and put Lockwood inside as gently as professionals would have done. He looked at the man with sunburnt hair and sideburns. "You got a name?" he asked.

The rangeman nodded. "Evan Turlock. This here is Bob Roberts. Are you comfortable?"

Lockwood was. They had been careful with him. When Lady Barlow came up and looked down into the wagon bed, she regarded Lockwood but addressed her riders. "Slow, watch for chuck holes. I got business at the bank. I'll see you at the yard."

There had been onlookers, not many but those who had witnessed Lockwood's being stowed in the Barlow wagon wasted little time in passing the word. The cafe man frowned as did Abel Starr and Billy Phelps. They weren't the only townsfolk who, knowing Lady Barlow, had trouble believing she had suddenly turned compassionate.

The ground was hard except in low places. The rangeman named Bob Roberts drove with full attention on the ground and expertly avoided bumps. Roberts was one of those individuals who did one job at a time and concentrated hard on doing it right. He had not said a word in town, and on the drive to the Barlow yard he did not say a word either.

Evan Turlock, his companion on the wagon seat, was older than either the driver or the passenger and seemed easy going, affable. He sat hitched half around so he could look down into the wagon bed. Two miles out of Derby he asked if Lockwood would care for a nip of pop skull. Lockwood accepted the bottle, swallowed twice, handed it back, and thanked the rangeman. Turlock did not offer the bottle to Roberts, who seemed too absorbed in watching for chuck holes to mind.

They were passing over some of the best grazing and browsing country Lockwood had ever seen. Fat mammy cows and sassy-fat calves watched the rig pass with cud-chewing curiosity. There were run-off creeks at lengthy intervals, *bosques* of white and black oaks. That recent deluge had reinvigorated growth. Rains, not heavy so much as warm and continuing, made all the difference between graze withering, going to seed early, and providing less strength, and continuing to flourish so that livestock came in at fall roundup fat as ticks with big, salable calves at their sides.

Evan Turlock still sat hitched half around, but he hadn't spoken for some time when taciturn Bob Roberts abruptly said: "What the hell is she thinkin' of?"

The barrel-chested older man's answer was consistent with his easy-going nature. "That ain't our concern, is it?"

Roberts should have been warned, but he wasn't. "A day wasted when we should be out with the others on the gather."

This time the easy-going man's reply was a trifle curt. "Bob, I've told you a hunnert times . . . ease up, take it a day at a time. She's the boss. We do what she says, an' win or lose it ain't our concern. Hey, the windmill's turning."

The Barlow buildings were made mostly of logs. They were weathered to a uniform shade of tan-gray. In a largely treeless area someone had planted trees many years earlier. They now provided a windbreak and shade. The barn was dominant. It had a loft above and stalls, granary, and harness area below. The bunkhouse was on the west side of the yard. Opposite it was a three-sided log equipment shed. Next to that northward was the smithy and beyond that was a cook shack.

Roberts warped the wagon close to the porch of the bunkhouse and was setting the binders when Evan said: "She'll want him at the main house."

Without so much as a questioning look, Roberts kicked off the binders, talked up the horses, made a half turn, and halted beside three wide steps leading up to the verandah.

The main house was also of logs. It was long and wide. The only indication that womenfolk lived there was a bed of flourishing geraniums on the east side of the steps.

As they climbed down to lower the tailgate, a dark woman with eyes the color of wet obsidian and the build of an oak stump appeared on the porch, drying both hands on an apron. She had pigeon-wings of gray over each ear; otherwise her hair was as black as the inside of a boot.

She stood impassively watching Lockwood being unloaded. She held the big front door. As Lockwood was carried past, he smiled. The woman did not smile back. She herded the men across a large parlor with a stone floor, down a wide, gloomy hallway to a room with white walls that reflected sunlight with doubled brilliance.

They put Lockwood on a four-poster bed of generous size, nodded to the expressionless dark woman, and went out, Bob Roberts first, Turlock behind him. The latter hesitated in the doorway to grin at Lockwood and jerk his head in the woman's direction. "She's got a tongue."

When Lockwood and the dark woman were alone, she asked if he was hungry. He was, but right at this moment other things were on his mind. He said: "I'm Cuff Lockwood."

The woman barely inclined her head. "I know. I am Francesca Santa Anna." She said it as though the two names were one. Santanna. She hesitated, then also said: "They call me Frank."

Her tone clearly indicated she did not like being called a man's name. Lockwood was not a tactful man even though it seemed that he was when he said, "If I was a woman, I wouldn't like bein' called Frank."

For the first time her dark features loosened and her gaze lingered on Lockwood. *Was it possible this unwashed, unshaven, tired-looking, nondescript human being could be different?*

He spoke again. "My first name is Saul.

Since I was a button, I've been called Cuff."

"Are you hungry?"

"No, ma'am. Maybe later."

"You need a bath."

Lockwood was learning. Francesca Santa Anna was totally outspoken. "It's been a while," he told her.

"I will give you a bath." The dark woman got as far as the door before Lockwood stopped her.

"I changed my mind. I'm hungry."

Francesca turned, impassive except up around the eyes. She was inwardly laughing at him. The next moment she was gone.

Shortly after his encounter with the Santa Anna woman, Lady Barlow returned. Lockwood could hear her spur rowels crossing the stone parlor floor. She had the stride of a man. He watched the door until she appeared. Every place Lockwood had ever been it was not just customary to remove spurs before entering a house, it was obligatory.

She had evidently left the braided quirt with her saddle. They exchanged a long look before she pulled over a chair, spun it, and straddled it the way men did. She tossed her hat on a carved marble-topped dresser, shook out her hair, and for a moment actually looked like a female.

"Did the bleeding start?" she asked.

Lockwood shook his head. He did not know whether it had or not, but he was not going to encourage an examination, something which had not bothered him with Bertha but which, for some reason, bothered him with this woman.

She had both arms hooked over the back of the chair. "Bob's a good teamster," she told him, referring to the taciturn man who had brought him here. "He just doesn't say much."

Lockwood nodded and waited.

"Is Frank fixin' you somethin' to eat?"

He nodded again.

She slightly cocked her head. "Nothing wrong with your tongue, is there?"

"No."

She smiled. It was a total surprise to Lockwood. He would have bet his horse and outfit she did not know how to smile. It altered her features. She had perfect white teeth inside that bear-trap mouth, and her steely eyes showed what Lockwood thought had to be an alien warmth.

"You'll be up and around directly," she told him. "Frank's a fine cook." The warm look faded. "She's the illegitimate daughter of the man who was president of Mexico, Antonio Lopez de Santa Anna. Not the only one. She . . . does not care much for men."

Lockwood said something that caught her entirely by surprise. He said: "Do you, Miz Barlow?"

She did not reply until she had arisen from the chair. "I'll tell Frank to hurry. Later, I'll visit you. Right now, I have enough work to keep me runnin' for a month."

When the dark woman returned with a laden tray, Lockwood had a question for her. "Seems to me, after thinkin' about it, I don't much like callin' a woman Frank. Do you have another name?"

She leaned to put the tray on a bedside table and did not look up when she answered. "My mother's name was Constanza. When I was half grown, she married a *gringo*. A man I loved very much. Worthless, he drank and rarely worked, but he was kind to us. He called my mother Connie."

Lockwood waited for her to look at him, but she didn't, so he said: "Would you mind if I called you Connie?"

Finally she straightened up, and their eyes met. She nodded once and left the room. In the wide gloomy hallway she stopped. *Why had she told him all those things? Because,* she told herself, *her heart had said for her to. He was different, but he still needed to be bathed and shaved.*

Evening arrived late, as it usually did this time of year. As yet there was no scent of autumn, but it was coming. The sky was flawless blue. Little chilly winds came and went. Leaves had not yet changed color, but they were beginning to curl.

Francesca came to light a lamp for Lockwood. She was silent until she had retreated to the doorway where she finally looked back and asked him if he had eaten well, something she already knew because the plates she had returned to the kitchen were completely empty.

He said it was true what Lady Barlow had told him, that she was a good cook. She left him without seeming to have heard, but later, when she brought him his supper, placing it handily close to the bed, she looked straight at him when she spoke.

"The sauce on those ribs came to me from my mother. She told me *gringo* men liked *salsa* to be both bitter and sweet."

When she returned much later to take the tray, he was waiting. "You're more'n a good cook, Connie, you're one of the best in the world."

She blushed and fled with the tray.

Lockwood was drowsy when he heard spur

rowels on the stone parlor floor and watched the doorway. Lady Barlow looked tired even by the poor light of Lockwood's oil lamp. This time she did not spin the chair. She dropped down on it, tossed her hat aside, and sighed. Her hair was an unusual reddish-brown. Tonight it was pressed to both temples with sweat.

She asked how he felt. He replied he felt much better than he had felt since being shot. He also told her Francesca was the best cook he had ever known. Lady Barlow nodded tiredly. She considered him briefly then said: "Wonders will never cease, Mister Lockwood. She told me she likes you, that you are a genuine *gente de razon*." At his bewildered look she clarified, "Gentleman of reason. That's a hell of a compliment coming from Francesca." She glanced out the only window, which was in the south wall. The way Lockwood was positioned on the bed, facing north, he could not see out the south window.

"Autumn's coming," she said, still looking out the window. "We'll be late making the cut this year. We're barely through with the gather." She slowly turned back, facing Lockwood. "Do you know what that means?"

He knew. "You'll be one of the last to

reach rail's end with your cattle."

She nodded. "The last ones get the least money."

He answered without thinking. "Next year start the gather earlier. That'll put you in the railroad corrals among the first. Maybe, if you do it right, the first."

She considered him briefly in silence. "If my foreman hadn't quit, maybe we could have done better. Next year we will. Well, I'm plumb tuckered. Good night, Mister Lockwood."

Bertha and Stuart Bentley, the cafe man, drove out to see Lockwood twice, once while he was still abed, the second time close to Christmas when he was able to be up without having recovered sufficiently to do more than go outside and sit in the chilly sunshine. The cafe man told him on their first visit that folks in town had lynched that son of a bitch who had tried to kill Lockwood from the dog-trot.

On their second visit Bertha told him the townsfolk had held a kangaroo court, fined the freighters ten dollars a head, told them if they ever returned to Derby they would be shot on sight — and were still holding that gunman the freighters had hired to kill Lockwood. The reason? They had discovered through a traveling man that Denton Middleton was wanted in Montana for three murders.

It began to snow in late December and did not let up until late February. Lockwood hated every minute of it. By March, with icy winds coming off the distant Tetons, he rode out with Lady Barlow's men to begin an early roundup for the purpose of branding and marking. As he told Lady Barlow, damned if her outfit was going to be last at the railroad corrals this year.

It was late spring with shy little flowers in the growing grass, bird song among treetops in the yard, and bulls beginning to drift off by themselves, that Lady Barlow went down to her bed with a lung sickness. They sent for the doctor, the same one who had made one cursory examination of Lockwood. He was disgusted to have made the long ride to find his patient up and around and never returned until he was sent for the second time.

His diagnosis was pneumonia. He agreed to stay at the main house until Lady Barlow got better. It was a long stay. He confided to Lockwood one evening, when they went outside to smoke, that while Lady Barlow was as tough as rawhide, as strong-willed as a rutting bull, pneumonia in someone her age could and very often did carry folks off.

That was the first time Lockwood had ever thought about Lady Barlow and age at the same time.

She recovered once summer was on the land. She had lost weight, about which Francesca fretted.

Lockwood was living in the bunkhouse when Francesca came to see him, wearing a *rebozo* that hid most of her face. It was a warm night with pinpricks of light the full width and length of a high-curving sky. Over the months they had grown close, something Lady Barlow had noticed and made several wry comments about to Lockwood.

This time she took Lockwood outside where they could not be overheard and told him Lady Barlow was drinking too much. Every day when she returned with the riders she had a large whiskey and water, and every night she now drank another tumbler full before retiring.

Lockwood hadn't noticed any difference in Lady Barlow. Only once had she called him to the house; that had been when the roundup was in full swing. She offered him as much money as he'd ever made in his life and the job of foreman. He had accepted.

Since then he had been too busy more than to wave to her when their trails crossed.

He listened to Francesca, was surprised at what she had told him, but said he was a hired rider. Lady Barlow's business was her own.

Francesca shocked Lockwood with what she now told him in a waspishly exasperated voice. "Men! You are so thick. Like oak. Why do you think she brought you out here last year?"

"Well, I was hurt and. . . ."

"¡Tonto! ¡Necio! ¡Simplon!" Her voice rose. "How can you have been here so long and not noticed?" Francesca made gestures with both hands. "She . . . was attracted to you. You never noticed? She . . . you didn't notice she did things with her hair? When she talked with you, she smiled?" Another fit of gestures came, this time accompanied with groans of exasperation and rolling eyes. "Mother of God you are *estupido.*"

Lockwood stood rooted. When the woman's fury began to diminish, he shoved both fisted hands deep into his pockets, unable to find words. She reached out, gripped one arm, and pushed closer to speak in a lower voice. "Listen to me, fool. She is a proud woman. What more could a proud woman do to attract you? Understand this. She would die before she would touch you first or say . . . soft things . . . to you."

The grip on his arm tightened. Francesca was surprisingly strong. "Help her! Not since her husband died has she needed someone's help as much as now."

"What can I do, Connie?"

She released his arm. "Take her buggy riding. It is summer."

"Connie, we're in the middle of the roundup."

She exploded again, waved her arms. She glared and said something in Spanish he did not understand. Then she gripped his arm again. "There are the riders. The best one is Evan Turlock. He was top hand for her husband. He can do everything. Do this much for her, *por favor,* I implore you."

She whirled and hastened back across the dark yard to the main house.

Chapter Ten

SHIPMAN'S ROCK

Lockwood did not sleep well that night. For a fact Francesca had completely surprised him. He *had* noticed small changes in Lady Barlow, but man-like he had been too preoccupied with ramrodding her cow outfit to consider a possible reason for those changes. Women did things like that — fluffed up their hair, put flour on their faces. Well, hell!

He was uncomfortable when he finally slept and awakened feeling the same way. As he went out front to breathe deeply of the fresh morning air, Francesca was standing on the porch of the main house, hands clasped beneath her apron, looking across the yard at him. The distance made it impossible to read her expression, but her stance spoke volumes.

He went out back to wash, met Evan out there, took him aside to say he wouldn't be riding out today, and left the easy-going rangeman looking baffled. He went back inside, changed into his clean shirt, looked at himself in the wavery mirror, ran bent fingers through his hair, and went out front. The sun was coming up. Birds were making noises in the treetops, and out back in one of the corrals a horsing mare shrilly squealed when a gelding approached.

Lady Barlow appeared on the verandah, tugging on her riding gloves. They stood looking at one another until Francesca said something to the other woman, and Lady Barlow stopped tugging on the gloves.

Lockwood felt like a fool. He went over to the foot of the verandah and asked if she would like to ride with him in the buggy after the men left. Francesca rolled her eyes. *Not only strong as oak but just as thick.*

Lady Barlow considered Lockwood for a long time. She was wearing a white shirt and her split doeskin riding skirt. She was booted and spurred.

Francesca leaned and spoke in a half whisper. Lady Barlow nodded at Lockwood, swung a booted foot to the porch railing, and removed one spur. She did the same thing to the other foot before speaking. "Is the gather coming along?"

"Yes'm. We'll start working them in a day or two."

Francesca was beside herself. They were like two cub bears fumbling a rubber ball. She cleared her throat, and this time when she spoke it was in her normal voice. "It would be good for you," she told Lady Barlow. "Too much saddlebacking is not good for women." She glared at Lockwood while speaking in the same gentle tone. "If the buggy is ready . . . ?"

"No ma'am, but I'll get it."

As he turned away, Lady Barlow's thick brows almost came together. She spoke to Francesca while watching Lockwood cross toward the buggy shed. "Why is he doing this?"

The swarthy woman's answer was soft. "Why not? He said the gather is ahead of time."

"But . . . ?"

"Ma'am, he is back to being a man again. Be pleasant with him."

Lady Barlow turned slowly to watch Francesca disappear inside the house. She went all the way to the kitchen before stopping, rolling her eyes heavenward, and saying aloud, *"¡Madre de Dios!"*

Lockwood side-lined the buggy horse across to the foot of the stairs. He looked up and smiled. "It's a real nice day."

He had crimped the forewheel so that her skirt would not touch the tire as she climbed in. She looked perplexed. As they were driving out of the yard, the riders were rigging out and turned to watch, their faces as expressionless as stones. Neither Lady Barlow nor Lockwood looked at them. But when they were half a mile out, she studied his profile, said nothing, and gradually relaxed.

They started up a covey of mountain quail. The harness horse did not even prick up its ears. Lockwood had no idea where they were going. Lady Barlow made that decision by suggesting they go northwest where she had seen a number of first-calf heifers.

He loosened, turned once to smile at her. She made a small, tentative smile back, but neither of them spoke until she pointed to some bedded cattle backgrounded by a *bosque* of second-growth white oaks.

"Their mothers used that as a calving ground. Sometimes I wonder about dumb cattle."

Lockwood could agree about that. "Take a sick critter to a corral where you feed it a couple of times a day an' it's seemed to me they show individuality like people."

She looked at him. She had noticed the same thing. A herd of cattle were just beef on the hoof. Taken separately they were definite individuals with distinctive characters and personalities.

The cattle came up to their feet, not as quickly for a buggy as they would have done for someone on horseback but just as warily. Lockwood drove around them at a fair distance. It was not possible to assess cattle if they were moving.

There were first-calf heifers in the band, but they had been calved out. There were no problem heifers. Lady Barlow gazed at the animals as she addressed Lockwood. "Why are we riding out here?"

"Nice day, ma'am, and the gather's ahead of schedule. I thought you might like the. . . ."

Her steely eyes came around to Lockwood. "Francesca," she said.

He became busy batting at a bee.

She laughed. It startled him. He had never heard her laugh before. The bee landed upside down on the roof of the buggy's top as he turned to meet her gaze and sheepishly smile. "I'll take you back, if you'd like," he told her.

She ignored the suggestion as though he had not made it. They left the *bosque* of spindly oaks, heading aimlessly northwest. When they reached a cold-water creek, he got down, removed the bridle and, as the horse tanked up, she looked at him from the shade of the seat and said: "Do you know where Shipman's Rock is?"

"Yes'm."

"Heifers lie up over there too."

They rattled across the creek in the direction of Shipman's Rock which had got its name because early-day trappers had rendezvoused there. It was a large, domed stone about twenty feet tall and massively thick. There was a creek nearby and trees. She told him the story of the trappers as they drove. Lockwood had always been a good listener.

When they came into the shade of the huge rock, she climbed down. He watched her stroll into rock shade and stand, looking back at him. She said something out of character for a woman accustomed to giving orders. "It's a pleasant place. If you'd like, you could hobble the horse."

He not only hobbled the animal, he stripped off the harness and flung it into the buggy. Horses, saddle or harness, had a bad habit of rolling when hobbled to graze. They had torn a lot of harness and skinned a lot of saddles that way.

He looked over where she was backgrounded by the big rock. Francesca was right. She had done something with her rusty-red hair. She was still built more like a man than a woman, but there was something definitely feminine about her now. It was her expression. Her mouth was relaxed.

Her pale blue eyes were not challenging. She stood with her arms behind her on the rock.

Lockwood went over into the shade. He could feel it. Something was happening between them. He plucked a long grass blade and chewed it, uncertain about a lot of things, and quiet.

She said: "I'm older than you are, Mister Lockwood."

He hadn't expected that. He would learn that she could put him off-balance at times. He spat out the grass stalk. "Are you plumb sure of that, Miz Barlow?"

"How old are you?" she asked.

"Thirty-five last winter."

"I'm forty-three." She gazed down across the rolling prairie. "It's been a long forty-three years."

He did not know what to say so he said nothing.

She returned her gaze to him. "Were you ever married?"

"No, ma'am."

She continued to study him over an interval of silence before speaking again. "I was married when I was sixteen. For more'n twenty years." Again she paused, and again he was silent, which she seemed not to notice. "We worked hard to build up the ranch and the cattle. Looking back . . . there were some things we just never had time for."

He could appreciate that. There were only three ways to get a large, prosperous cattle outfit — inherit it, marry it or, as she and her husband had done, work every day long hours year in and year out.

"We started the bank in Derby an' bought buildings in town." She gazed at him thoughtfully. "After my husband died, it seemed like half the men in town would ride out to visit." She made a quirky little smile at him. "Even some married men."

That was reasonable. A wealthy woman with a big, prosperous cattle outfit. He plucked another blade of grass. Doggone Francesca. He liked Lady Barlow's company — now, anyway, when she seemed human — but he had never liked folks telling him their affairs.

She leaned back on the big rock. The shade was surreptitiously moving a few inches at a time. Lockwood looked up. The sun was farther off center than he had expected it to be. They should start back directly.

"Just never had time," she said abruptly.

Lockwood looked out where the harness horse was going down in front, then in back, stretched out, rolled over and back three times. He said: "Three hundred dollars."

She swung her head, saw the horse arising to stand spraddle legged while it shook, and laughed. She had been jerked out of her reverie. There was a saying that for every time a horse could roll over and back he was worth a hundred dollars.

"Tell me about yourself, Mister Lockwood."

He spat out the grass stalk. "Well, to start with I been with you over a year now. Most places I've worked before, that much time passed, folks used first names."

She nodded. "Cuff. Tell me about yourself, Cuff."

"Not much to tell, ma'am. I've worked most of the north-country ranges."

"Your parents?"

"They homesteaded. The third year, when they was ready to prove up, the cholera took them both. . . . I had a good horse, so I struck out. The rest of it's about like it is with most rangemen, one job after another, one trail after another."

"And you never married?"

"No," Lockwood stated and had a fleeting moment of discomfort. "Once I met a girl. It was springtime. That was some time back. I rode on."

"No brothers or sisters?"

"No. Just me."

Lockwood's discomfort was increasing by the moment. He rarely talked about himself. He had told Lady Barlow more than he could remember ever telling anyone. He had nothing to hide. It was just that he did not like recalling painful memories. They began with the death of his parents.

She took him by surprise when she said, "It's not natural, Cuff. You should marry."

He blushed, felt annoyed, and faced her. "You got any suggestions, ma'am?"

Her answer this time struck him speechless. "Me."

She walked briskly out to the horse, removed the hobbles, and led it back to the buggy. She got the harness, flung it over the animal's back, and did not once look in the direction of the big rock.

Lockwood came over in time for her to hold the shafts while he backed the horse between them. She then buckled on the right side while Lockwood did the same on the near side. They climbed into the buggy. Lockwood flicked the lines. Lady Barlow sat beside him, looking straight ahead.

They were back at the first creek where he had watered the horse that morning when he stopped as though to alight and spoke without looking at her or moving to get out of the rig. "I thought men was supposed to ask women."

She remained stiff, looking straight ahead as she replied. "They are, but at my age it don't pay to wait."

He climbed down, looked in at her, and burst out laughing. She faced him, smiling. "You looked like you was about to faint."

He stopped laughing to say, "I dang near did."

When they were heading southeasterly in the direction of the Barlow yard, he sat forward with slack lines as he said, "Am I supposed to answer right off?"

"No. When my husband asked me, I ran into the house and told my maw. She was tickled pink. I went to my room and cried."

He flicked a horse-fly off the harness animal's rump with the lines. "I don't think Evan an' the others would understand, besides it's been a long time since I cried."

She surprised him again. She jabbed him in the ribs with her elbow. It didn't hurt, but it did something else. It established a touching relationship.

He eased back against the leather cushion and thought it might be nice if this day, particularly this buggy ride, never had to end. He hadn't smoked all day. Now, he handed her the lines, dug for the makings, and methodically rolled and lighted a cigarette.

She said, "That's something else I've missed. I like the smell of tobacco."

So her husband had smoked. Francesca would undoubtedly tell Lockwood anything he asked about her husband. He tipped off ash and said: "Miz Barlow . . . are you really serious?"

She swung her head. "Dead serious. More serious than I've ever been in my life."

"I could be a drinker," he told her and got back a curt response. "That's all right. I don't really care for the taste of it, but I'll drink right along with you."

He finished the smoke, snuffed it out, and pitched it into the grass as they came in sight of rooftops and tall old unkempt trees. It was easy to be with her now, so he checked up the horse and turned. "I always figured folks kissed first, then asked about gettin' married."

She reached with both arms. Her kiss was gentle at first, then clinging. When it was over, she did not look away. She said: "Cuff, it's been so long I wasn't sure I'd remember how. I can see Francesca standing on the verandah."

He talked up the mare with eyes pinched

hard. He could also see Francesca on the verandah under the overhang. He wagged his head. If they could see her, sure as hell she had seen them.

As they were entering the yard, she said: "Please don't call me by my first name. That was my mother's idea. She was so dead-set I would be a lady she gave me that name. My father called me Toby."

He grinned. "T'tell you the gospel truth that Lady business always gave me trouble . . . Toby."

She reached and squeezed his arm. In a low tone she said, "Does that mean . . . yes?"

The riders were not in yet, but Francesca had not moved as they wheeled over to the equipment shed, and he crimped the wheel for her to alight. But she didn't. She sat with both hands in her lap, waiting.

He climbed out, looked back, and said: "I'm hungry."

She glared, climbed out on the opposite side, and said, "Francesca will give you rat poison," and started across the yard.

He took his time removing the harness, backing the rig into the shed, and leading the horse across to the barn to be cuffed before she was turned out and fed. He burst out laughing. The horse turned her head to stare. He led her out back, turned her into a corral, went over to the trough, and sluiced off. He had sweated harder today than he usually did after a hard day of labor.

Chapter Eleven

INDELIBLE MEMORIES

Shortly after Christmas they were married, not in Derby, but in the big, stone-floored parlor of the main house. When the news first reached town, it surprised folks. Not everyone thought it would last. Lady Barlow was hell on wheels, had been since her husband's passing. Bertha and a few others, who had known her before his passing, were ambivalent. She had been strong-willed, even then, and capable, but she had also been much less assertive and sharp-tongued.

On the wedding day, when Abel Starr came by for Bertha driving his best top buggy hitched to a chestnut mare fat enough to shine in the pre-spring sunshine, Bertha climbed in, looked at the burly livery man, and tartly said: "You trimmed your beard."

Abel drove north out of town as he nodded but did not speak.

She leaned, sniffed, and said, "Where's your cud?"

"I give it up," Abel stated, not sounding happy.

Bertha twisted to stare. "You quit chewin'?"

"I just said that, Bertha. Are you gettin' deef?"

"Will wonders never cease."

They left the road, heading northeast over cold ground. In places the buggy horse's shoes rang over ice. Abel, who was wearing a string-tie that made him almost as uncomfortable as the suit coat that bound his shoulders, said: "People are supposed to get married in June. Look at that sky."

Bertha looked. "Clear blue as far as I can see."

"Cold," Abel stated. "There'll be a rind of ice on every trough in town come morning."

Bertha had to hold her elegant little hat as they bumped across a pair of old ruts. "Abel, you're off your feed," she said.

He still sat hunched forward, holding slack lines as he turned his head. "He's out of his mind. A man'd have to be to marry Lady Barlow. She's just plain cantankerous. I'll lay you a bet, Bertha . . . ten dollars gold it don't last a year."

She resettled the hat before answering. "The livery business must be good. That's a lot of money."

"You want to bet or not?"

She tapped his arm. When his head came around, she said, "Go back to chewin' Abel, your disposition is goin' to ruin this day for me. It'll last. Take my word for it. I know Lady Barlow better'n you or anyone else in town. The side of her you've seen is the side she shows all men."

"An' she won't show it to Lockwood?"

Bertha sat back, watched the big trees and log buildings coming closer, and sighed. She said nothing more until they had left the rig and were mingling.

More than half of Derby was there, faces shiny from scrubbing, dresses ironed, pants and coats smelling powerfully of moth balls. The preacher was one of those itinerant Bible-bangers who showed up like falling leaves. He was a paunchy big Mormon who no one would see for months after the wedding as he would have long since moved on in his search for lambs to save from Satan.

There was a roaring fire and cider in bowls. It was at least thirty degrees hotter in the parlor than it was outside. When Lady Barlow came up out of the gloomy hallway followed by Francesca, folks stopped dead still. She was still as flat chested as a boy, but her gown was as beautiful as had ever been seen in the Derby countryside. It should have been; it cost a hundred dollars from a mail order company in Chicago.

Her face was radiant. The pale eyes were soft. The bear-trap mouth was relaxed and full. Bertha nudged Abel. "You got a handkerchief?"

He fished for a blue bandanna, handed it to her, and scowled. "If you caught cold ridin' out here, don't blame me. I'll get you some cider."

She felt for his sleeve and locked her fingers. "Stay right here," she hissed.

Lockwood came in from out front. Francesca had coached him. It wasn't decent for a man to see his bride until just before they were to be married. He stopped just inside the doorway, blocking the way for Evan, Bob, and the other two riders. Lady Barlow's eyes met Lockwood's gaze across the room. He took root until Homer Westphal, the banker, who was standing nearby hissed from the side of his mouth: "Go ahead. Don't just stand there!"

Evan nudged Lockwood from behind. He started toward the fireplace where the preacher was waiting and sweating — the fire behind him was hot.

Lockwood had never in his life owned a pair of britches and a coat that matched. Bertha and Barry Grant, who owned the mercantile in Derby, had made the selection from a catalog and were both surprised when it arrived — and fit. Lockwood had never before worn a necktie in his life and, like the livery man, was uncomfortable with the one he now wore on his white shirt.

His boots had been cleaned and greased. He looked presentable by most standards. When the paunchy big preacher in his rusty suit — used only for marryings and buryings — got them positioned in front, he opened the Good Book and began a lengthy preamble about the sanctity of the holy ceremony of marriage between folks. Stuart Bentley, the cafe man, let his gaze drift to the cider bowl. It was hotter in the parlor than the hinges of hell. Beside him Andy Lipton, the saloonman, leaned slightly and whispered. "It won't take long. That fireplace is fixin' to melt him."

Lipton was right. The preacher left off two-thirds of his usual preamble and got down to the marriage vows. The entire ceremony only lasted about fifteen minutes. The first one to move afterwards was the preacher. He sidled clear of the fireplace.

Men came forward. Lady Lockwood turned her cheek to be kissed. Bertha blew her nose. Stuart turned his back and reached for a cup beside the bowl of cider. Francesca cried unabashedly, which seemed to be a signal for a chain reaction. Every woman in the parlor cried while the men milled uncomfortably.

Lockwood kissed his wife. Her eyes were misty when she smiled at him. She made a remark that would be the source of their relationship down the years. She said: "Honestly, Cuff, I'd about given up hope."

He winked at her.

The crowd lingered until shortly before sundown, which came early this time of year. When they departed, the Lockwoods went out to the verandah to thank them, exchange jokes, and watch the steam when the horses began moving. There was a two-thirds moon in a sky without a single blemish. It was going to be colder than a witch's bosom that night.

Francesca was cleaning up when they went outside. Lady Lockwood left the room to change before returning to help Francesca, who cornered her in the kitchen and glared. "This is your wedding night!"

"I'm not going to leave you with all this mess."

"*¡No mi importa un comino!* Go! He is on the porch. *Go! Go!*"

She went. Lockwood turned when she appeared in the cold night. He was smoking and trickled smoke as he looked at her. She said: "I had to change and help Francesca."

He froze her in her tracks when he said something she had not heard in about twenty years. "You are beautiful, Toby."

She went close, placed both palms on his upper chest, leaned, and kissed him very softly. When she stepped back, she was almost solemn. "I was afraid."

"Of what?"

"Several things. You. You might change. Not all men are . . . well . . . marriageable."

"You told me I should be married," he said.

"I meant it. You are a handsome man." She went to lean on the verandah railing, facing him. It was not only cold. It was also shadowy under the overhang. He looked very young. So did she but the thought did not enter her mind. She smiled a little. "I suppose every woman has misgivings. I did when I married at sixteen. I was also frightened."

"And now?" he asked.

"I'm not frightened . . . well . . . not in the same way, but I am worried. Cuff?"

"What?"

"I have a terrible disposition. Anyone will tell you that."

He put his head slightly to one side as he

gazed at her. "Toby, I've worked for you over a year. I've seen you mad." He grinned. "Everyone gets mad."

"You don't. I've never seen you angry."

His grin broadened. "Give me time, Toby." He held out a hand and she took it. Her fingers were like ice. He tugged her off the railing, held the door for her and followed, then closed the door. The heat was less than it had been when the room was full of people, and no one had put a log on the fire, but it was still warmer than necessary.

He filled two cups with cider, handed her one, and raised the other in a little smiling salute. "To a long life . . . and the day you get mad an' I take you down a notch."

They emptied the little cups. In the kitchen Francesca was making noises with dishes, pots, and pans. She was also humming. Neither of the people in the parlor recognized the song which was just as well. Mexican *canciónes* were almost invariably about lost love, sad partings, the anguish of affection.

She said: "And you, Cuff, being a married man . . . ?"

He considered her thoughtfully. He had seen all her moods but not this one, not uncertainty, not self-doubt. "I told you how much I cared. We've gone on picnics. I've held you, Toby. We sat in the grass at Shipman's Rock and beside creeks. I've told you that loving a woman was a scary feeling with me. I've also told you it's an overwhelming feeling." His eyes crinkled when he also said, "Tomorrow the men an' I start marking an' branding."

Her eyes widened, then narrowed. She had learned something about him: he teased. But for a moment she could not think of a single appropriate answer so she slowly smiled. "Not tomorrow. Tomorrow we won't even open our eyes until noon."

Francesca appeared in the kitchen doorway with shiny cheeks. "It is late."

Toby Lockwood nodded. "Go to bed, Fran . . . Connie . . . you were wonderful. I owe you so much."

Francesca blushed, threw them both a roguish look, and went back into the kitchen. It is always so beautiful at the beginning as anyone knows who has been married three times. Sometimes it never stops being beautiful, who can say? Once it was for her; twice it was not beautiful very long. The first time . . . and he rode away with *pronunciados* and never returned. So the beauty had ended. It became tears in the heart, but they were — and still were — beautiful.

A wolf howled close to the yard. Lockwood cocked his head, listening. Toby ignored the racket. There were always wolves, particularly in winter. Someone slammed the bunkhouse door. It was a very clear sound in a hushed, cold night. Lockwood started for the door. His wife almost called him back, checked herself in time, and heard him go down off the verandah, heard him call to someone in the night, heard a voice she recognized as belonging to Evan Turlock reply, then silence.

She went to the bedroom, touched her wedding gown with gentle hands, shook out her hair, turned down the lamp, and went to stand by the window in her night gown.

He would return of course, but there would be other abrupt departures. It had been that way with her dead husband. It had also become habit with her since his passing; there was always something that needed immediate attention. While people slept, other creatures, like wolves, were awake.

Wolves had always been a nuisance but mostly during calving time. There were stars like diamond ships to watch and, on a night as clear as her wedding night, there seemed to be thousands of them, and the night was so still, no wind, not even a breeze.

She knew what that meant. In a day or two a late snow. Cuff disliked snow. She turned toward the bed. He had been on his way down to New Mexico. That had been almost two years ago. He had not said one word to her the last couple of winters when he'd had to be out in four-foot drifts with two feet on the level.

She thought back. There were other things she had known he had not liked. He had never mentioned them. She thought even farther back, to his shoot-out in front of the cafe and when he had been ambushed across from the saloon.

She very clearly remembered the first time she had seen him. It had been a dismal day in spring. He had been coming out of the cafe. There had been another man come out, a sallow-faced individual wearing a black hat, and it had been raining.

Someone out front called. Not words, just a shout. She was jarred out of her reverie waiting for the answer. When it came, she unconsciously loosened. The voice was Lockwood's. He clearly said: "In the morning, Evan. Good night."

She dropped her eyes and smiled only with her lips. Not in the morning.

When he returned, came down the wide old hallway, drawn by the light, she waited until he entered the room, then said, "Did you find him?"

He sat on the edge of the bed as he kicked out of his boots and was reaching to loosen the tie when he fully noticed her. He answered but in an indifferent way. "Yeah. It was a bitch wolf. Shrunk to skin and bones. We could have run her down."

"You didn't shoot her?"

"Toby, she's got pups somewhere. She was too shrunk to make much milk." He stood up to shed his coat and shirt. "She went out a ways when she heard us coming, stopped, and sat there waiting. It . . . I never saw a wolf do that before. Neither had Evan. She sat there, looking straight at us."

"Was she sick?"

"No. She was starved. I talked to her while Evan went back to the bunkhouse for some meat. She never moved nor took her eyes off me. It . . . I wanted to pet her. You know what I think?"

"No."

"She knew she couldn't feed her pups, figured they would die, so she was ready to die too." Lockwood stopped undressing. "I know how I'm sounding. You've heard In'ians say they can talk to wolves without makin' a sound? That's how I felt. Evan brought back two handsful of meat left over from supper. He put them down an' we walked back and turned to watch."

"She ate it?"

"Every scrap an' licked the ground. She looked at us a while then turned and trotted away into the night." He finished undressing. "Toby, I think we got a new member of the family."

"The men will shoot her. Someone will, Cuff."

"Not here they won't. Evan's goin' to explain."

"Someone will. If she came this close to the yard here, she'll do it somewhere else."

She stood gazing at him, thinking of things she had heard since childhood, most recently from Francesca. It was in the stars that for every wedding night there was an omen.

She smiled at him. "I'm glad you fed her."

He blew down the lamp mantle. The sheets were like ice. He stiffened for a moment. It had seemed he heard a wolf cry from a great distance.

His wife said: "What is that on your left shoulder in back? I can't see it very well, but I can feel it."

"A birthmark."

Chapter Twelve

AN INTERRUPTION

Lady Lockwood gradually became what she had once been and, since the death of her first husband, had longed to be again: a wife, a homemaker, a woman whose existence was totally involved around a man. Lockwood worked hard. For five straight years Barlow cattle were first at the railroad corrals.

The sixth year Bob Roberts broke his leg at the knee joint when a horse fell with him. He was bedridden for three months. When he could stand again, the knee was stiff. Lockwood gave him what pay he had coming and three hundred dollars in an envelope. Evan drove Roberts into town. When he returned, he told Lockwood the taciturn rider had said of all the outfits he'd ridden for and of all the range bosses he'd taken orders from, Barlow ranch was the best and Lockwood was the fairest and most decent.

They hired a man named Stevens to replace Bob Roberts. He was a good hand but young. One chilly autumn day when Lockwood and Evan Turlock were hunting strays, wrapped to the gills in their coats, Evan made a remark about something Lockwood had not thought.

"They're gettin' younger, Cuff."

Lockwood gazed at his companion. Over the years they had become close. Until this bleak autumn day Lockwood had not noticed that Evan's hair was thinning and the lines in his ruddy-complected face were deeper.

When he got home, shed his coat and hat, Toby met him in the soft-lighted parlor. He would have sworn she did not look any older than the first time he'd seen her. He had come to recognize something about her over the years. Her mouth was softer. Her eyes didn't challenge a man. He told her what Evan had said, and she smiled. In that weak light Lockwood did not look any older to her, either. But Francesca was heavier and slower although her hair was still mostly as black as a crow's wing and her face was remarkably unlined.

Winter arrived and passed. Lockwood's deeply ingrained dislike of snow remained, but as a particular part of his life it was no longer dominant. He winter fed with Evan and the new man. He worked at the early spring gather and later at the autumn round-ups, feeling no different. He rarely even thought about time passing. They had increased the cows and had imported pure-bred red-back bulls with barrel-shaped bodies, short legs, and horns not as long as a man's forearm.

Each springtime calving, the calves were smaller at birth which meant fewer heifer deaths from hung-up first calves. Those same calves came in during autumn two hundred pounds heavier than before they had bought the pure-bred bulls.

Bertha Bradley had married Abel Starr, the livery man. He had sold out the livery business and for the past six years had been tooling coaches for the new stage company in Derby. He and Bertha had been married most of those six years. Unlike some women, as Bertha had aged, she hadn't gotten heavier, she had gotten thinner. Toby came back from town one day in late summer to tell Lockwood a secret. Bertha had sent away for an elixir, and now her hair was dark brown without a strand of gray. They had laughed about that.

Later, returning from the drive down to rail's end with the sell-off, Lockwood, Evan, and the other two Barlow riders, both younger men, stopped at Andy Lipton's water hole after supper down at Stuart Bentley's cafe, and Lipton brought them a bottle and four glasses without being asked. A tall man with hair half way to his shoulders leaned forward and said: "He's gettin' deef-er'n a post."

Stuart came in from the cafe. He did not look different except that he was now little more than bone and sinew, but he had never been much more. His dark complexion was slightly darker, but Lockwood did not notice. The cafe man'd always been swarthy. Evan repeated what the long-haired man had told them. Stuart rolled his eyes. "He's been gettin' that way for years, but it's a sore subject with him." Stuart nodded as Lipton brought another glass. As he was heading back up the bar with all the men watching him, Stuart also said: "There's nothin' wrong with his memory. He knows what everyone drinks and sets it up for 'em. Where he runs into trouble is when strangers come along." Stuart raised his glass. "Mister Lockwood . . . Evan . . . your health."

As the cafe man put his jolt glass aside, he looked at Lockwood. "Too bad about old Silas, the harness maker."

Lockwood thought he knew what was coming but asked anyway. "What about him?"

"He died in his sleep couple months ago. There's a new feller at the shop now. Feller named Todd Snelling. He's good, better'n old Silas ever was."

Lockwood leaned against the bar, turning his little glass in its sticky dampness. He recalled the time the old harness maker had called to him at the exact moment that bushwhacking son of a bitch had shot him from the dog-trot.

Abel Starr came in, pulling off his stager's high, smoke-tanned gauntlets. Lockwood was shocked. Abel was as gray as a badger. Otherwise he looked and acted the same — big, bluff, and hearty.

On the ride back to the ranch Lockwood said little. He had never been an individual who thought in terms of hours or years. He worked from sunup until sundown. He had responsibilities that allowed little time for reflection, and except for a memory that occasionally bothered him and which concerned that dream he hadn't had now in many years, he lived a day at a time, from season to season, from springtime markings through summers of moving cattle from short feed to taller feed, from the fall gather to the drive at rail's end.

He was never ill and rarely ached. Toby's fondness for her husband had increased over the years. They had been married for fifteen years when she came down to the corrals where her husband and Evan were roping on foot as a pair so the other, younger hands could dump calves, worm them, cut horns that were little more than buttons to make sure they would never grow, and leaned on corral stringers, watching.

Lockwood was a good roper. No matter which way a calf bolted, he could move his body for unfailing casts. Her first husband had once told her a scrap of range wisdom she remembered. Mostly, ropers cast depending on whether they were right handed or left handed. A right-hand roper could miss a cast if the critter was running to the left. Some ropers were good with either cast, but they were rare. Lockwood was one of the rare ones. Evan was an old hand. Being right handed he would jump at a calf running to his right. It would wheel and dash to the left. Evan never missed. As Toby watched, she smiled. Evan had learned to compensate.

They were not only close, but they understood each other better, she thought, than a lot of wives understood husbands or husbands their wives.

When they stopped for a breather, she saw Evan lift his hat to mop sweat, and her eyes widened. Evan had always had light hair, not brown and not quite blond. Where sunlight hit it, his light hair was lighter now — it was solid gray, almost silvery gray.

The following summer the Lockwoods and Evan drove into Derby for Barry Grant's funeral. Barry had founded and operated his Derby Mercantile Company for almost thirty years. His wife stood at the open grave with a tiny handkerchief to her face, but she did not openly weep. She was a small, plump woman, gray and lined. She had, like Bertha Bradley, been a friend to Toby Lockwood back in the days when she had been Lady Barlow.

Barry Grant had friends. About two-thirds of the townsfolk were out there, intermingled with cowmen from the countryside. The minister, properly solemn in matching black coat and britches, belonged to the new church in Derby. In fact he had built the structure almost single-handedly, except for what volunteer labor he could dragoon. He was a youngish man, broad shouldered, barrel chested, and likable. After the funeral he put Grant's widow into his buggy and drove back to town.

Ezra Evans, retired from the town smithy for eight years now but still arrow straight and muscular, came over to the Lockwoods and said: "You folks don't get to town much, do you?"

Lockwood agreed. "It's not like it used to be, Ezra. The ranch takes all our time . . . an' more if we'd let it."

"Did you meet the preacher?"

They hadn't. The blacksmith wagged a finger. "It don't pay to put off things like that too long."

On the way back to the yard Evan tugged his tie off, pocketed it, and said: "I've known Ezra since he first come into this country. I never knew a man who could cuss for three minutes without repeatin' himself like he could. I guess folks change when they're on the sundown side, eh?"

That was the year they lost seven head of loose stock to horse thieves. Lockwood sent Evan to Derby to tell the constable, a long-legged beanpole of a man with freckles and odd-colored, sort of tan-gold eyes. His name was Reginald McDuff. Where he had come from, in Missouri, folks had called him Duff. In the Derby country they called him Reg.

He promised to come out, try to pick up the sign, and track down the thieves. When Evan got back, he took Lockwood aside and repeated what the constable had said, shook his head, and frowned. "He don't have to *try* and find tracks. Hell, they're plain as day. Cuff, there was three of them. I'd guess they got maybe a five, six hour head start."

Lockwood pondered. "Did he say when he'd be out?"

"No. That's the point, Cuff. Them bastards are movin' fast. If he don't come out until tomorrow, he might as well not come at all."

Lockwood gazed past his top hand in the direction the thieves had gone — northward toward the distant mountains. Without looking back he said: "Make up a pouch of grub, fetch your Winchester. I'll meet you at the barn in a few minutes."

Evan nodded. "Just us two?"

Lockwood grinned at him. "There's only three of them, ain't there?"

His wife and Francesca were toiling at bread vats in the kitchen when Lockwood went through the house for his coat, an extra carton of bullets for his Winchester, took the weapon from its corner of the bedroom, and turned. His wife was standing in the doorway.

"Is the constable coming?" she asked.

"If he does, tell him Evan an' I are trackin' 'em."

She did not clear the doorway as he started for it. "Cuff, we can stand losing seven horses."

"Toby, next time it'll be ten. After that twenty."

"Take the other men with you."

He shouldered around her with the Winchester in one hand, his sheep-pelt-lined rider's coat in the other hand. He pecked her on the cheek. "There's only three of them," he told her and hurried from the house down to the barn.

As he and Evan Turlock led their saddled animals out front to be mounted, they saw both women, Lockwood's wife and Francesca, standing like statues over on the verandah. They waved, rode northward out of the yard at a walk, veered northwesterly until they picked up the tracks, then followed them at a slow lope.

From the sign it was clear the thieves had set the horses into a hard run, which was to be expected. Evan squinted ahead. The tracks did not deviate. They went straight toward the distant mountains.

An hour later, still slow-loping, Lockwood pointed and said: "They're scuffing, Evan."

His companion's response was curt. "They got to be new at the business. Anyone with a lick of sense knows you can't set horses to a dead run an' keep them at it."

The scuff marks had been made by horses who dragged their feet from exhaustion.

They loped steadily across open country. Lockwood guessed that by now the horse thieves were into the yonder distant foothills. Up there, the horses would have to be rested. Mountains were not made for riding fast.

Lockwood rolled and lighted a smoke. He passed the makings to Evan who looped his reins and also rolled a smoke. The sun was listing on its downward course from the meridian.

They came upon a mare heavy with foal who was standing head hung. They passed her at a lope. She barely more than glanced at them. Evan made an observation tinged with scorn.

"Greenhorns as sure as I'm settin' up here. No horse thief would take along a heavy mare. In fact, no real horse thief would steal loose stock without first spendin' a day or two pickin' out the ones worth stealing."

By the time they were close to the foothills, where the tracks went unerringly toward higher country, dusk was approaching. Tracking in daylight was not difficult, not when the sign had been made by seven horses, and it could be done at dusk, but not very easily at night unless there was a clear sky and a full moon. The sky was clear enough, but the moon was little more than a thin crescent.

They dismounted and led their horses. For as long as any light was available, they could read the sign but, once they left the scrub-brush foothills for timbered high country, they could do no more than move very slowly, watching for churned earth. It did not help that the timber was old growth, massive and tall, with treetops cutting off what little light there otherwise would have been.

Evan never lost his contempt for the thieves, not even when Lockwood halted in a small clearing and tethered his horse as he off-saddled and hobbled it. Evan did the same. The last bit of gear they removed were the bridles. Their animals hopped out where grass was tall but didn't graze along. They ate in one place the way only very hungry horses do.

Evan produced the pouch of food from the bunkhouse. They squatted and ate. After they had finished eating, Evan left Lockwood to the horses, disappeared through the trees, was gone about an hour, and returned looking thoroughly disgusted as he said: "A fire about a mile ahead."

They left the horses, took their carbines, and started walking. Lockwood eventually saw reflected firelight and nodded when Evan said: "Damned idiots."

It wasn't hard going, although the land sloped uphill, but the farther they went the thicker, more dense the big trees became. Once, when they stopped, Lockwood made a guess. "They didn't drive all seven horses up in here. Hell, a top hand couldn't keep 'em together in here."

Evan had an even more pointed remark to make. "Crazy, anyone runnin' for it like they was back yonder would just naturally turn east or west an' stay out of the damned timber."

By the time they could smell smoke, they could no longer see the fire, but they did not have to see it. A solitary bay horse with the Barlow horse brand on his left shoulder came picking his way down country. He either didn't scent or see them because he kept right on walking, passing within about two hundred feet of the motionless watchers.

From this point on they moved slowly without making a sound. A light breeze came up country. They could no longer smell smoke, but they were finally close enough to see the shifting reddish shadows being reflected off trees.

Lockwood halted beside a forest giant. He could make out loose horses and shook his head. By morning, without hobbles, all the horses would be back down in open country. The only thing that kept them up here right now was exhaustion.

Evan growled a sour groan as they inched closer with as much distance between them as the trees made necessary. Closer, they heard firewood crackling. This near they could also make out three hunched figures around the fire.

Evan slipped down beside Lockwood. "One of us can beard 'em, the other one'll stay hid for support."

Lockwood nodded, and Evan began inching his way among the trees to be hidden from the men at the fire until he was ready to challenge them. Lockwood also crept forward, leaving enough room between them for Evan to spring the surprise. One of the hunched silhouettes abruptly arose and went toward the nearest big tree. He had his back to the others, who ignored him. One horse thief was smoking. The other one was lolling back, evidently fed and confident. This one spoke to the smoker.

"Losin' three ain't bad for the kind of country we're in."

The smoker's retort was cranky. "I told you . . . we should bring along hobbles. But you said. . . ."

"What in the hell are you complainin' about? We still got the others."

"We could have kept all seven."

"Not that heavy mare."

"Six then."

The man who had gone out to pee returned, sank down, and was rummaging a ragged old coat for the pocket with a plug in it when Evan spoke without raising his voice. "Put your hands straight out in front. *Do it, gawddamn you!*"

The smoker lost his cigarette. All three of them jerked erect and put their arms in front at full length.

Evan walked out of the trees holding his six-gun at his side. He stopped near a tangle of saddlery, raised the gun so that they could see him, and cocked it. "Reach under them coats real slow and toss your weapons away. Slow now." He moved the cocked six-gun slightly from side to side covering all three horse thieves.

They obeyed during a period of utter silence except for the crackling fire. Evan looked at the guns they tossed aside and raised his voice slightly. "Cuff. The horse-stealin' business don't seem to pay much. Look at them guns. One of 'em's an old black-powder hawgleg. The others are almost as bad."

Lockwood came forward with his Winchester held low in both hands. He stopped behind one of the seated men, pushed a cold

Winchester barrel against the back of his neck, and said: "Stand up. Don't turn, just get up."

Very slowly the horse thief arose. Across the fire Evan made a startled curse. "Hell! You other two stand up. Don't get yourselves killed, just get up, and don't move."

Lockwood walked around where Evan was standing and got the same surprise Evan had got. He eased down the Winchester's dog, grounded it, and spoke to the horse thief nearest him. "How old are you?"

There was no answer until he fiercely swore and repeated the question.

The nearest horse thief said: "Thirteen."

Lockwood jutted his jaw at the horse thief directly opposite him. "You! How old are you?"

"Sixteen. That there's my brother . . . he's a year older'n me. He's seventeen."

Evan went among them, roughly searching. They had no other weapons. He punched the oldest horse thief as he growled for him to sit back down. All three of them sank to the ground.

Lockwood hunkered with his Winchester for support. He and Evan exchanged looks until Evan said: "I told you . . . damned poor professional horse thieves."

Lockwood asked the youngest horse thief

where they came from. The answer was made in a small, frightened voice. "We come from up north near Perkinsville."

"Is that where you stole the horses you're riding?"

"Yes sir."

"Where are your folks?"

"We don't have no folks."

"None of you?"

"No sir. We run away from a foundling school where the law put us after findin' us hidin' in a man's barn at Perkinsville."

Evan came closer and sat down with the Winchester across his lap. Lockwood offered the makings, which Turlock took and rolled a smoke which he lighted from a burning stick. While Lockwood was making his own smoke, Evan scowled menacingly at the oldest boy. "Did you ever see a man hung?" he asked.

The youth shook his head.

"But you know that's what happens to horse thieves, don't you?"

"Yes sir."

Lockwood lit up during the silence that followed Evan's statement concerning the fate of horse thieves. The youngest boy turned a dirty face with pale blue eyes and a tipped-up nose. "Was they your horses, mister?"

Lockwood nodded, trickling smoke. "Where were you goin' with them?"

The middle youth, who had not spoken until now, answered. "There's a trader up at Perkinsville that buys horses."

"Did he say he'd buy stolen horses?"

"No sir. We never talked to him. We just stole three of his horses and headed south to find some to steal."

Evan looked pityingly at the speaker. "You were going to take our horses up yonder to sell to a man you stole three horses from? How old did you say you was?"

The sixteen-year-old boy was ragged with bad teeth. He was no taller than the thirteen-year-old. He lowered his head without answering.

Evan looked over at Lockwood. "I'll go back, bring up the horses. We can hang 'em an' be home in time for breakfast."

The youngest boy's eyes filled; his mouth quivered; he dug in the ground with his fingers. The two older boys sat like stone carvings staring into the fire. The youngest one could not hold it back any longer. He began to sniffle.

One of the older boys looked at him. "I told you if we got caught they'd. . . ."

"You never said no such a damned thing! You said if we did it right . . . in the dark an' all." His sobs made further conversation impossible.

Evan stood up. "I'll fetch the ropes."

Chapter Thirteen

RIDING BACK

Lockwood watched Evan disappear in darkness among giant trees and sat impassively, thinking that Evan would indeed bring up their horses, but what he'd really done — knowingly — was leave Lockwood to make the decision. Evan was no more in favor of hanging children than Lockwood was, but it would be up to Lockwood.

The oldest boy finally broke the silence. He didn't whine, but he sure-Lord pleaded. "Mister, we never done this before. We just figured somehow we had to find a way not to be hungry all the time . . . an' get run off when we went around askin' for food. We walked a long way goin' to ranches along the way. Maybe some of 'em would have hired me, but they wouldn't hire on all three of us, 'specially no thirteen year old. Mister, we didn't mean no harm. We had to do somethin' to keep alive. Mister . . . we give you our word we'll never steal no horses again."

Lockwood sat like an Indian with fading

firelight on his face, motionless, silent, thoughtful. "You had folks," he eventually said.

The youngest one stopped sniffling. "My maw died of the lung fever an' she never tol' me who my paw was. I made a grave an' buried her up north."

"Where up north?"

"Outta Laramie, southward, near the Colorado line. That's where she give out an' died."

"Who helped you dig the grave?"

"No one. There wasn't no town or nothin', just some railroad tracks and open country."

"Where'd you get the shovel?"

"I didn't have no shovel, mister. I used sticks an' my hands."

"Where did the three of you come together?"

The oldest boy answered. "Perkinsville. My brother 'n' me met . . . him . . . in a potato cellar where we went during a snow storm."

"What about your folks?"

The answer struck Lockwood like a dagger. "They died of the cholera four years back."

Lockwood asked no more questions for a long time, not until he could hear Turlock coming, then he said: "Horse stealin' will get you hung. You knew that, didn't you?"

The middle boy nodded. "We talked about it. Mister, you ever been hungry?"

Lockwood did not answer. He was listening to the approach of a ridden horse and a led horse.

The youngest horse thief got hiccups trying to be as manly as his companions and not blubber. But his eyes ran. He brushed a ragged, soiled cuff over his face. He alone looked defiantly at Lockwood. His companions kept their heads lowered. The fire was down to coals. Chilly night air was creeping in. Lockwood picked up some dead-fall limbs the horse thieves had gathered, pitched several onto the coals, and squinted when flames erupted.

Evan came out of the night with the coiled lariats off the two saddles. The boys watched him without seeming to blink as he squatted beside Lockwood and went to work methodically building a smoke.

The youngest horse thief again lost his struggle. His body shook with sobs he could not entirely control or stop. Evan lit up, looked at Lockwood, and smoked. By firelight he began fashioning slip-knot hang ropes with both lariats. One of the older youths bit his lip until it bled. The other one suddenly spoke in an unsteady voice, repeating something from his past. "The Lord is a shepherd an' I won't be scairt."

Lockwood and Evan exchanged a look. Evan stopped working with the ropes and pitched his smoke into the fire as Lockwood spoke to the horse thieves.

"I don't expect your words are worth a damn but, if you get caught doin' this again, you won't ride off. Give us your words you'll never steal horses again."

The boys sensed a chance, and each one gave his word. Lockwood ignored the abrupt change in the horse thieves. He arose, looking down at them.

"Right up until now, if you're caught again stealin' horses, that's how it'll be. The next time you'll get hung as sure as I'm standin' here."

Evan arose with the lariats. He leaned to expectorate into the fire, leaned back, and said: "You got guns an' there's game in the mountains. We're goin' to take your horses to make up for any of our own we can't find."

They left the horse thieves sitting at the fire. Lockwood rode easterly. Evan rode southerly. When they met down near the scrub-brush foothills, they had nine horses. With daylight coming, they picked up the heavy mare and let their loose stock shuffle toward home at their own pace.

Lockwood said: "You don't expect they'll sneak back down an' steal back their horses, do you?"

Evan laughed. "I'll bet a month's pay no one ever sees 'em again on this side of the mountains. Cuff?"

"Yeah?"

"Did you ever know youngsters who was like those three?"

"I knew one, Evan. You?"

"Yeah. I knew one, too."

It was mid-morning before they corralled the horses, cared for their own animals, pitched hay all around, and parted in the center of the yard. Evan headed for the bunkhouse, Lockwood for the main house.

Toby came from the kitchen where she and Francesca had been working over big pans on the wood-stove preparing to put up wild grape jelly. They had been at it all morning with no more than an occasional word passing between them. Entering the parlor, Toby wiped both hands on her apron. Lockwood shucked out of his heavy coat, leaned the Winchester aside, and opened his arms. Toby asked if they had caught the horse thieves. Lockwood escorted her back into the kitchen, which was pungently fragrant and hotter than a forge fire, sat down, and told them all that had happened. Francesca placed a cup of Irish coffee before him.

Toby made breakfast, and Lockwood ate every bit of it right down to the flower-design on the plate. He left them, went to the bedroom, kicked off his boots, draped his shell belt and holstered Colt from the back of a chair, stretched flat out on the bed, and slept until late afternoon.

When he awakened, he did not move for a long time. Gazing steadily at the ceiling, he was oblivious to everything, sounds from the kitchen, from the yard where the men were noisily helping a down-mare have the foal which had not been due for another three weeks, even bird song from the verandah's overhanging eaves where nesting was in progress. Every year it was the same, barn-swallows who built mud nests, created new nests beside their last-year nests as though some bird law prevented them from reusing perfectly good last-year nests.

He hadn't had the dream for years, hadn't forgotten it but, as the years passed, he had thought less about it. This time it was more vivid than he recalled it ever being before. Her face was almost expressionless with tears slowly coursing down both cheeks. She had simply looked steadily at Lockwood. Other times she had softly smiled, as he remembered her smiling, or she was profiled, sometimes with her head slightly to one side as though she was listening to something — or maybe *for* something. This time she neither blinked nor changed expression; this time it was the face of a woman whose heart was breaking.

He went out back to the wash house, pumped the zinc tub full of water, gasped when he first got in, then sat there ignoring the cold for a long time. Eventually he scrubbed, climbed out, toweled off, pulled the plug for the water to drain outside, and shaved. His hair needed shearing; it was almost completely gray. He looked at himself in the wavery mirror seeking additional signs of aging. If they were there, the wavery glass obscured them.

He dressed in clean clothes, solemnly combed his hair, and returned to the house long enough to pull on his boots before going out onto the verandah to roll a smoke. The day was dying. Shadows from the big old scraggly trees made pock-like shadows on the barn. The bunkhouse had a spindrift of smoke rising straight up in the still warm evening.

He was still sitting out there when dusk

settled and his wife came to tell him supper was ready. He ate in almost total silence. Francesca and Toby exchanged a look. Francesca rolled her eyes, turned her back to the table, and filled a large pan with hot water from the reservoir on the side of the stove, exactly as she had been doing for more years than she could recall.

Lockwood returned to the verandah for his after-supper smoke. Tonight that spindly crescent moon was fatter. Last night it had shed practically no light. Tonight its glow softened the darkness. One of the riders was playing a mouth-harp at the bunkhouse, being accompanied by another rider who was playing a Jew's harp.

Toby came out wearing a light shawl, sat down near Lockwood, and did not say a word. She listened to the music, identified the song as one that had been popular on both sides during the Civil War: "Lorena," a sad song of a man's thinking of home, dark nights, and uncertain tomorrows.

Lockwood could see her profile in the gloom. As before in soft light, she looked like a girl. Even the silver in her rusty-red hair did not show.

He began slowly. "Before I came to Derby, I met a girl on the range near a town called Dunstan. She was settin' in a shady place beside a little creek. I didn't see her at first. I watered my horse . . . and there she was. It was the best time of year. Grass comin' on, birds, warm ground. . . ."

Toby sat perfectly still, looking straight ahead.

"Afterwards I rode on."

"That's when you came to this country?"

"Yes."

"That was a long time ago, Cuff."

He told her about the dreams, about the latest one, how clear her face was with tears on the cheeks. Toby continued to sit erect facing around. She knew what was coming, and it did.

"It hasn't come back for a long time, Toby, but this time it was clearer than it ever was before. She was cryin' about somethin'."

"What do you want to do, Cuff?"

"I don't know what to do. It was like she was tryin' to say something."

Toby shifted slightly on the chair but still did not look at him. "Do you remember the wolf, Cuff?"

He hadn't thought of the starving bitch wolf in fifteen years. "You mean the night after we got married?"

"Yes."

"I remember."

"Do you know what Francesca would say about your dream?"

"I expect so. She sees omens. Over the years she's told me."

She turned to face him. "Do you still love that girl?" she asked.

"Toby, I didn't *love* her. She was pretty an' all, but I didn't love her. I didn't even know her."

Toby's gaze was unwavering in the gloom. "You're no more superstitious than I am. But things happen it's hard to understand and impossible to interpret. Cuff, go find out. She's been trying to tell you something."

"Toby, they're dreams. In'ians believe in them things, we don't."

She looked steadily at him. "We don't know everything. No one does. I've dreamed most of my life, but mostly I couldn't remember them come morning. Cuff, go find out. If it's nothing, come back." She leaned slightly toward him. "It's important to you. She'll haunt you as long as you live, unless you go back there."

He busied his hands, rolling and lighting a smoke for which he felt no need. He let the smoke trickle fragrance until it died unnoticed. "What do you mean . . . if it's nothing come back? This is my home. You are my wife." He gestured with the hand holding the dead quirley. "Toby, this is my world. I love it, an' I love you. I'll always come back wherever I go."

She faintly smiled in the gloom. "What I meant was . . . go back to Dunstan. Stay as long as you have to. I know you'll come back. What I meant was . . . go settle this thing with her."

"Toby, what could I say to a woman I met once . . . years ago?"

She gave a delayed reply. "I have no idea." She leaned farther, caught his hand, and gripped it. She wanted very much to tell him not to go; she was afraid without being able to define what she feared.

"Do it, Cuff. I love you more than you know, but you have to do this."

He returned her grip. For moments they sat like that until she freed his hand, and he sank back in the chair. "That's what I've been worrying about. Going back there. I know that's what the dream was about."

They sat a long time in silence. The lights went out down in the bunkhouse. Behind them Francesca turned down a table lamp in the parlor and went off to bed. The night turned chilly. Toby snugged up in her shawl but until her husband leaned to arise she sat still.

He stepped to the edge of the verandah, gazing out into the night. Behind him she arose, brushed his arm with her fingers, and said: "Get an early start. The sooner you leave the sooner you'll come back."

They went inside. She blew down the lamp mantle in the parlor before following him to their bedroom. Soft, almost eerie, moonlight came through the south wall window. They bedded down in silence. Neither of them slept until along toward the wee hours, then she slept as he arose, dressed, took his coat, his Winchester, and went silently through the house to the yard and down to the barn. It would be another hour or two before Evan and the other riders awakened, but by then he would be on his way.

He did it this way on purpose. He hadn't wanted any farewells nor had he wanted to ride away in daylight when he would be able to see everything behind him that had been his life for so long. Better in the dark when he could hear nothing, see nothing.

It was cold an hour or so before dawn. He rode hunched into his coat, riding a trail he remembered well enough despite the years which had passed. When daylight came, he was at the outermost limits of the Barlow range. From that point on he rode by instinct. From time to time he thought he recognized land marks. By the end of the first day he had recalled things he hadn't thought about in years. It was like riding back in time.

The second day he met a swarthy man who smiled and was very pleasant and spoke a language Lockwood could not understand and was not sure he had ever heard before. The stranger had a small band of sheep, several dogs, and a pair of feather-legged big gentle horses to pull his home which was a wagon with a stovepipe sticking up from a rounded top. There was a whole inventory of items hanging on the sides of the wagon, including a washboard, three collapsible canvas buckets, some coyote or wolf traps suspended in a bunch by their chains, and drying sheep pelts which were being scoured on their undersides by big blue-tailed flies.

Lockwood had known in years past of wars between sheepmen and cattlemen. This particular Basque shepherd neither wore a gun nor had seemed the least bit upset when a rangeman rode up. Maybe those differences had been settled. In the Derby country there were no sheep — but times were changing.

He and the swarthy man shared a meal and laughed a lot, neither able to understand the other. When Lockwood rode on in the morning, he gave the Basque a ten dollar gold piece, which seemed to shock the shepherd. In his world guests were making an insult if they offered money for hospitality.

Lockwood covered many miles and did not bed down until after dark when he came upon a cold-water creek with good graze on both banks. He went to sleep listening to his horse eat — about as pleasant a sound to doze off to as a man could hear.

He encountered cattle the following day and some landmarks he had no doubt about having seen before. It was a slow and gradual process, but the farther he rode, the closer he got to Dunstan, the fresher his memory became. It was almost like rolling back about eighteen years, almost like being young again.

The country had changed, but since he'd never known much about it, had just ridden through and in fact didn't know the town at all, he could only tell what was new from what was old by the condition of fences, the smoke from distant buildings where wagon ruts were not deep.

He had been on the trail six days. He might have reached Dunstan sooner if he had hastened, but only the fact that he was going there seemed important to him, not how quickly he arrived. He reached the outskirts in late afternoon, put up his horse at the livery barn, visited for a while with the livery man, a grizzled older man with sore feet who walked like a duck and never any farther than he had to. His name was Alexander. He told Lockwood folks around town called him Alex. He never did mention whether he had a first name.

They stood out front looking up through town until the livery man went to a bench, sat down, and offered Lockwood a crooked, dark little Mexican cigar, which Lockwood declined as he sat down to roll and light a cigarette.

Alex was garrulous. He seemed to know everyone in town. He also seemed to know their business. He told Lockwood he was a widower. Lockwood incorrectly assumed Alex was an old-timer in the Dunstan country. He learned otherwise when he asked about a family named Harrison. Alex furrowed his brow, squinted at the dust in front, and slowly shook his head. "I know of 'em," he said, "but I only been in these parts ten, twelve years. They had a big cow outfit northwest of town, over along Cottonwood Creek, but they was gone before I come here. As near as I know, there's some markers in the graveyard with that name on 'em."

Chapter Fourteen

SEARCHING

Dunstan had changed too, but never having been there before, Lockwood could only guess what was new and what was not by the condition of buildings, and by the number of people. Like the town he had come from, when he had first arrived there, people were not scarce but neither were they as numerous as they had become over the years. He thought this was probably true of Dunstan, and for a fact Dunstan had several businesses Derby still lacked. A telegraph office, for instance, and a seamstress' shop. A new church but also a physician.

There was an abstract office run by a gnome with pale skin, no hair on top, and who wore glasses with lenses as thick as the bottom of a whiskey glass. His name was Alberston, and folks called him Al. He was a friendly gnome. If he was remarkable for anything, it was his height. He was no more than five feet tall, and had a habit of removing his glasses to wipe slightly bulging pale, watery eyes.

Lockwood met the abstract man the day after his arrival. He also met the man who operated the local hotel which was new enough so that, when the sun was on the west side of the building, sap oozed and flies got trapped in it. He was young, a little more than half as old as Lockwood. He had a dowdy little pregnant wife that, mouse like, never ventured out if she could avoid it. She, too, had pale skin. Like the man who ran the land office, she was pale as a ghost.

The younger man's name was Spearin. George Spearin. He had been in the Dunstan country four years and had come there from West Texas, which he told Lockwood had wind when no place else on earth had it and too damned much heat.

Lockwood settled into a clean room with a window facing south down through town. Afterwards he went in search of a tonsorial parlor. He'd needed shearing before leaving home. The barber was old, at least ten years older than Lockwood, and talkative, which seemed to be a requisite for people who cut hair and shaved folks. Lockwood listened to local gossip for a while then asked the old man if he'd ever heard of the Harrisons who used to have land and cattle somewhere west of town.

The old man snipped, squinted, trimmed

until he was satisfied, and said: "Yes sir. I knew old Jake Harrison real well. Right up until he sold out and moved away, I trimmed his beard and sheared him regular every two months. It was a terrible thing happened to 'em." The old man left off snipping for a moment. When he went back to work, he said: "Jake and his woman didn't deserve it. No sir. They was decent law-abidin' folks who worked hard, never had bad words about nobody." He stopped again to squint at Lockwood's hair before stepping close and continuing his work. "There was a feller . . . dead now . . . name of Jefferson, a real hell-raiser. He didn't fear gawd nor man. He was sweet on Shelly Harrison, their daughter. After what happened to her, he searched high an' low to kill the man who done that to her. Never found him. Jefferson died a few years back when a stagecoach goin' north went around a mountain pass too fast, hit an ice slick, and went over the edge . . . three hundred feet. Killed 'em all, horses, driver, an' Jefferson."

Lockwood asked about the girl. The old man clipped furiously for a moment, then put his shears aside, used a brush to sweep loose hair off, and raised his bottle of French toilet water to sprinkle when Lockwood raised his hand. "Leave that be," he told the old man, who shrugged and put the bottle back on a shelf. Most rangemen liked French toilet water. It made them smell pretty.

The old man removed the cloth so Lockwood could get out of the chair. He did this with a flourish as he continued speaking. "The girl? Gawd punished her for sinnin'. She died a-birthing."

"Was she married?"

The old man looked up through his thick lenses. "No, she weren't married. No man'd marry a female already with foal."

Lockwood handed the old man silver, left the shop, went as far as a bench in front of a dry-goods store, and sat down. People passed; some nodded; some smiled. Lockwood saw none of them. He eventually arose and stopped a portly man with a massive gold watch chain across his middle and asked directions to the cemetery.

The portly man gave specific directions and turned to watch Lockwood walk away. Strangers weren't unusual in Dunstan but strangers were who wanted to know where the cemetery was.

It was a beautiful day. There was a hint of a soft breeze. The sun was climbing. The farther he walked the more the sounds of Dunstan diminished.

The cemetery was on a low hill inside an

iron fence. It was shaded by huge old trees. It was about half a mile from town to the northeast. Cattle were grazing outside the fence. There was a top buggy parked near the gate, which had been left ajar, someone's oversight, but the rig was in front of the gate so the cattle did not come close.

An old man and his frail wife were sitting on a stone bench. He had a hat in his lap. The frail elderly woman was dressed entirely in black, even to the little hat atop her gray-white hair.

They ignored the stranger when he passed. Not until he had walked back and forth among stone markers did the old man look around. Lockwood had hardly more than noted them sitting there. The old man leaned to speak to his wife. "He can't find it, Mary."

She nodded without looking away from a grave. She tucked a tiny handkerchief in her purse and arose. "It's time to go, Robert."

He too arose. "Maybe I can help him."

She nodded in a disinterested way. "Yes. Maybe you can. I'll be at the buggy."

The old man waited until Lockwood came closer as he read headstones. The old man cleared his throat. When Lockwood looked up, the old man spoke in a kindly voice. "Maybe I can help. I knew 'em all one time or another." He paused and nodded in the direction of the grave where the old man and his wife had been sitting. "That's our boy. He died seven years back." The old man cleared his throat again. "If I can help . . . ? What's the name you're lookin' for?"

"Harrison."

The old man's watery, faded eyes widened a tad. "Shelly Harrison?"

Lockwood nodded.

The old man put on his hat and stepped out into sunshine as he raised an arm. "Yonder, under that big cottonwood tree." He dropped his arm, thought a moment, then murmured to himself: "A shame, mister. A real shame. She was such a lively, nice girl. It like to killed her folks. After they put her down, they sold out an' left the country. I don't know whatever become of 'em but me 'n' my wife used to be friends with 'em. I guess it was the shame of it."

Lockwood said: "Thanks," and left the old man, who watched Lockwood make his way among the rows of stone to the cottonwood tree. His wife called. "Robert. Come along."

The old man shuffled toward the gate, although once he stopped to look back.

The tree was tall with limbs that needed trimming. It shaded half an acre of stones and grass. Lockwood stood motionless even after the top buggy drove off in the direction of Dunstan.

He sat on the ground beside the grave. It hurt to read the stone, which simply said:

Here Lies Our Beloved Daughter,
Shelbourne Harrison.

There was a date for birth and one for death. Below the dates was an inscription.

The Lord Giveth
The Lord Taketh Away
He Forgiveth Sin

The last line impaled Lockwood like a knife. *At the time . . . young men don't understand the consequences . . . it was springtime, the sap was running, the ground was swelling with new life.* He closed his eyes and relived every vivid moment.

He sat there until dusk. After he closed the gate, stood a moment looking back, his heart ached and his throat was squeezed closed with pain.

He got back to Dunstan with shadows forming, with lights on both sides of the main roadway, with a few people strolling, and a number of dozing horses at the tie rack in front of the saloon. The cafe was only three shops south of the hotel. People were entering and departing. At the lower end of town carriage lamps had been lighted on each side of the wide barn opening of the livery barn.

Lockwood had never been much of a drinking man. He still wasn't, but a fleeting thought arrived. He banished it while standing on the porch of the hotel. He had never found peace at the bottom of a bottle.

He sat on the porch with the town alive around him, was still sitting there when most of the lights had gone out and the man who owned the hotel came to lock his front door, saw the motionless dark silhouette in the chair and called to him. "Time to lock up, mister."

Lockwood arose, pressed past the younger man, went to his room, lighted the lamp, turned it down, and stood by the window. When the last light was doused, he went to the bed, kicked out of his boots, draped his shell belt and weapon from a wall hook, and lay on his back atop the blankets.

Sleep would not come, nor did he expect it to, nor care for it to particularly. He recalled her face as though he had last seen it the day before. Her smile. She'd had a dimple in each cheek and eyes the color of corn flowers. She had been soft and warm.

He left the bed to stand by the window again. He might have been angry with himself, and ashamed. What he felt was a kind of pain he had never felt before. A sense of loss, of guilt, of loathing for the young Lockwood who had gotten on his horse and had ridden on.

The older Lockwood thoroughly disliked the younger Lockwood. When he returned to the bed, he eventually slept but not comfortably nor very well.

Before daylight he was down at the livery barn where Alexander was asleep in his horse-sweat-scented little combination office and saddle room. He was sleeping in a rickety old swivel chair which had twisted wire beneath to keep the legs in place. And he snored, choked, cleared his pipes, and snored louder than ever as Lockwood saddled up, led his horse out back before mounting, and rode northeasterly in pitch darkness with a distinct pre-dawn chill which he scarcely noticed.

He had only a vague idea where the Harrison ranch was — the buildings and yard anyway — but he could recall every creek-willow, every mound, every sound of birds where he had stopped to water his horse eighteen years earlier.

He rode without haste. He hadn't ridden

any other way since he'd left home. He had felt no need for urgency. He still felt the same way. He had returned. He was here. He had to find the place where he had swung off to water his horse, that was all he had to do. It was all he felt impelled to do.

He missed the place by a mile, did not realize it until dawn came, and he was atop a land swell, approximately where he had been when he'd seen the creek long ago. It was down there, unchanged, still with willows lining both sides of the waterway. He corrected his course, came down off the land swell exactly as he had done the only other time he'd been in this country, rode slowly toward the creek, held up one arm to ward off willow limbs as his horse crossed the creek, rode clear, halted, and swung down. He turned slowly. Everything was the same.

He hobbled the horse, pulled off his rig, upended the saddle in the grass, draped the bridle over an upturned saddle skirt, and straightened up, facing away. He had done exactly the same things before. He did not turn for a long time, but when he eventually did — he was alone.

There were birds, even some bees. The creek made its busy, hurrying sound. He went back to the place where they had been, sank down, pulled up both legs, encircled them with his arms, and stared over an immensity of land with the sun in his face.

His throat hurt. His eyes misted. He locked his jaws and waited for the almost overpowering surge of anguish to pass, which it did as the sun moved higher.

Later he rolled and lighted a smoke, eased back in the grass, tossed his hat aside, and waited for the anguish to diminish. If she had wanted him to return, he had done it. If that was all she had wanted. . . . He killed the quirley. There was no way he could tell her how he loathed the young rangeman who had spent an exquisite afternoon with her. Maybe she could, somehow or other, feel what he was feeling. Maybe that would be enough for her.

As Toby had said, there's more we don't know than we do know. He fell asleep soundly and serenely and did not awaken until his horse nickered. It was dark, that strengthening moon he had left behind about a week back was getting thicker, closer to being full. He sat up. The horse was standing like a stone, ears up, looking intently into the southwesterly night.

Lockwood stood up, dropped the hat atop his head, and tugged loose the tie-down thong that prevented his holstered Colt from falling out. The night was utterly still and silent. Hair was rising on the back of Lockwood's neck until he heard them, a band of foraging coyotes no more than a hundred feet from him.

The horse hobbled a few jumps and stopped, peering and listening. If it had been daylight, it would have been possible to see him shaking.

Lockwood went over beside the horse, put a calming hand on its neck, walked ahead, and fired his six-gun. The horse hopped frantically. The coyotes yelped and continued to yelp as their racket became fainter.

Lockwood went back, bridled the horse, removed the hobbles, saddled up, and stood a moment to have a cigarette for breakfast before mounting and heading back the way he had come. Again, in the dark, he would not have to look back, exactly as he had done when he left home a week or so earlier.

It seemed to take longer to reach Dunstan than it had taken to get out there. Riding in the night always made distances appear longer than they were.

Dawn was breaking when he entered the livery barn from out back, leading his horse. Old Alexander was nowhere to be found — for an excellent reason, he was having breakfast at the cafe, which was as far as he walked and wouldn't have walked that far if he'd had a stove at the barn and knew how to cook.

By the time Lockwood had cared for his animal, the old man came duck-walking down the runway. He called a greeting, disappeared into his saddle room, and reappeared as Lockwood was walking toward the roadway. He said: "Wait a minute, mister," and duck-walked faster until he came up close, then looked around, saw an upended empty horseshoe keg, and sat on it.

He considered Lockwood for a long moment before speaking. "Ain't none of my business, friend. But someone stopped the southbound stage a few miles north of town last night, robbed the passengers, and made off with a money box comin' down to Mister Thompson's gen'al store." Alexander produced a lint-encrusted plug, gnawed off a corner, pouched it into his cheek, spat once, and spoke again. "Like I said, friend, it's none of my business . . . you just havin' come to town, an' took your horse sometime last night, an' was gone up until now. . . ." Alexander spat again, then he smiled. "I'm just tellin' you because the town's like a hornet's nest. You bein' gone last night. You see what I'm getting at?"

Lockwood gazed at the old man and nodded. "And you figure I'd be wise to saddle back up and ride on?"

"Well, it might be for the best," the old man said and spat again.

Lockwood's gaze did not waver. "An' suppose it was me, Mister Alexander?"

The livery man shifted slightly on his little keg, looked up the roadway where sunshine was dazzlingly bright, and did not look back when he spoke. "Like I said, mister, it's none of my affair one way or the other." He finally returned his gaze to Lockwood. "But I can tell you this . . . Dunstan's got a mean-tempered town marshal. If anyone seen you leave town last night. . . ." Alexander made a gesture with both hands.

Lockwood asked where the marshal was and got a predictable response. "He left out of here with a burr under his blanket about sunrise. But he'll be back, friend. You can bet on it. He'll be back."

Lockwood went over to the cafe, which had two steamed-up windows, walked in, and was nearly deafened by excited diners yelling back and forth. He ordered breakfast, shucked his gloves, pocketed them, and eased his hat back. He did these things as naturally as he always had. He did not notice the conversation diminishing as the cafe man fed him. Once, when he looked up, he caught the other diners staring at him. They immediately looked elsewhere. It did not dawn on Lockwood until he was out front that he had been the only man in there wearing a rider's heavy coat, the kind rangemen used in bitter cold weather, or when they had been riding in the night.

Chapter Fifteen

THE TAIL BACK

Lockwood went to his hotel room, shed his hat, shell belt and holstered weapon, took a towel and a worn chunk of tan lye soap, and went out to the wash house. He took an all-over bath and afterwards shaved. He heard someone outside and ignored it. The hotel owner had a bean and squash patch. Someone was probably hoeing weeds out there. It was that time of year. Most townsfolk raised vegetables to be bottled for winter food.

He dressed, opened the door — and froze. There were four of them with shotguns. One was the cafe man. Another was the young man who owned the hotel. Lockwood recognized another man, the individual he had asked for directions to the cemetery, a paunchy man with pale skin and a massive gold watch chain across his middle.

It was the paunchy, pale man who addressed Lockwood. "Walk around the side of the house, mister . . . hands away from your sides."

Lockwood's astonishment held him in the wash-house doorway. The cafe man, a narrow-faced, weasel-eyed individual swore as he hauled back the hammer of his shotgun. *"Walk, gawdamn you. Move!"*

They marched him down the main thoroughfare toward the jailhouse. People stopped to stare. A pair of rangemen passing on horseback did not stop, but they craned around until Lockwood was in front of the jailhouse then decided against leaving town after all, reined over to the saloon tie rack, and swung off.

The Dunstan jailhouse was not new. In fact it had once been a crib, but the separate little rooms had been turned into strap-steel cages. The hotel man motioned for Lockwood to sit on a bench. His four captors seemed confused about what to do next until the cafe man told Lockwood to empty his pockets, which Lockwood did, piling the contents on the bench at his side. There was another troubled pause. Lockwood gently shook his head at them, which annoyed the sharp-featured cafe man whose scattergun came chest high, aimed squarely at the man on the bench.

"You think it's funny, don't you? Well, it ain't, an' when the marshal gets back, you'll find out how funny it is. What's your name?"

"Cuff Lockwood."
"Where you from?"
"A place called Derby, about a week's ride southeast of here."
"What're you doin' in Dunstan?"
Lockwood eyed the four of them. Over the years he'd ridden with posses, but this was the sorriest bunch of law-and-order individuals he had ever seen. They not only did not know what to do, they were nervous as cats on a tin roof.
The sharp-featured cafe man spoke again, more irritably this time. "I asked you what brought you to Dunstan?"
Lockwood returned the weasel-eyed man's gaze without blinking. "It's none of your damned business why I'm in Dunstan."
The sharp-featured man yanked back one of the dogs on his shotgun. The paunchy, pale man growled at him. "Aim that gawd-damned gun somewhere else, Ellis." The paunchy man jerked his head at Lockwood. "On your feet an' through that door."
They locked Lockwood in a strap-steel cage and went back up front, slamming the door on the cell room. Lockwood went to a wall bunk, sat down, and rolled a smoke. They hadn't told him why, and they didn't have to. Lockwood remembered the looks he had gotten at the cafe, and the earlier

warning from the livery man. Why he was in Dunstan was something personal and private. He wasn't worried as much as he gradually became indignant. Those silly sons of bitches.

The paunchy, pale man came down to stand in front, looking at the prisoner. "Mister Lockwood, a stage was robbed upcountry last night. A money box was taken that was to be delivered to my store. An' the passengers an' driver was robbed." The pale man paused with a faint frown on his face. "I went down to the livery barn. You ride a real nice animal, an' your outfit's better'n most rangemen got. Tell me somethin', does that town you mentioned have a telegraph office?"

Lockwood smiled a little, ruefully. "No. The nearest telegraph is about sixty miles south in a town called Agua Caliente." Lockwood arose and approached the front of the cell. The storekeeper was a head shorter than Lockwood. Of the four vigilantes, or whatever they called themselves, the storekeeper was nearest Lockwood's age and seemed nearest to sharing Lockwood's temperament.

He shook his head at the prisoner. "Well, you picked a hell of a time to come here. That's all I got to say. We're goin' to keep you locked up until the marshal gets back."

Lockwood accepted that. "An' suppose he comes back with your highwayman?"

"It'll be a relief to me, for a fact. The whole town's in a turmoil, an' now we got you in here, folks are actin' even worse." The paunchy man wagged his head. "Right or wrong I've never seen the town so roiled up. Hell, you'd think it was their money box instead of it bein' mine." The storekeeper was momentarily silent before he said: "Two thousand dollars," turned, and went back up to the front of the jailhouse, closing and barring the door from the office side.

It was much later, in fact it was evening, before he heard someone up in the jailhouse office. It was three men arguing. One of them sounded louder than the others, and angry. Lockwood couldn't distinguish words, just voices.

He hadn't eaten since morning. Cigarettes helped with some things, like keeping a man awake, but they did nothing for an empty stomach. And his sack of smoking tobacco was almost empty.

The loud argument abruptly ended. Moments later someone yanked open the cell-room door and came stamping down the dingy, narrow corridor. Lockwood's first look at Dunstan's town marshal gave him an impression that would never change. He was tall, rangy, needed a shearing, had a cud pouched into one cheek, and glared in at Lockwood from dark brown eyes.

He wore his six-gun low and tied down. Lockwood recalled what Alexander had said about the marshal being mean tempered. He turned from beneath the high slit of a window in the back wall of the cell and walked closer to the front as the rangy, dark-eyed man spoke.

"I'm Jess Duffy, town marshal." He let that hang in the air between them for a moment before speaking again. As he spoke this time, he leaned forward, inserted a large brass key, and unlocked the cell door. "You can go." He then blocked the doorway. "What's your name?"

"Cuff Lockwood."

"What's your business here, Lockwood?"

For a moment Lockwood considered the same answer he'd given to the weasel-faced man, then changed his mind, and said: "Ridin' through."

Marshal Duffy remained in place, blocking the doorway. "Might be a good idea if you rode on. The town's upset about you." This time, when the rangy man paused, he seemed to have trouble forming his next words. "Dunstan owes you an apology."

Then the gruff voice rose a notch. "Them damned idiots. I'm the law here. They ain't. They was lucky they got an unarmed man. Next time . . . I told 'em, the damned fools . . . next time they'll jump the wrong man an' get theirselves killed."

Marshal Duffy stepped aside. Lockwood preceded him up to the office, nodded, and left. It was dark out. He went up to the hotel. The proprietor was nowhere around, but Lockwood met his timid, little, mousy wife. She said her husband might not be back until late but, if Lockwood wanted to pay up and leave, she'd take care of it for him.

Lockwood thanked her, brushed past, entered his room, which had been roughly searched, took out his Colt to see if the loads had been removed. They hadn't. He stood by the window for a while, watching lights go out around town, left the hotel, went down to the cafe, and walked in as the owner was filling sugar pots on the counter. The cafe was empty.

The sharp-featured man's expression froze. He watched everything Lockwood did, saw that Lockwood was not wearing a sidearm, and loosened slightly as he said: "Mister . . . well, everyone makes mistakes, don't they?"

Lockwood nodded, walked to the counter,

and with two feet of wood between them said: "Where's your shotgun?"

The cafe man shuffled back a foot. He had a sugar pot in one hand, a dipper of sugar in the other. "It's in the back room," he murmured, getting paler by the moment. "Mister, you got to admit . . . the coach bein' robbed last night an' you comin' in here this morning like you'd been out all night . . . ?"

Lockwood did not raise his voice. "If I was you, I'd get rid of that shotgun. You're too nervous to own one. Twice you cocked that thing in my direction."

"I just told you, we figured. . . ."

Lockwood's arm came up to the shoulder and shot straight ahead. Sugar went one way, the cafe man went the other. There was a slung-back thin streak of blood at the corner of his mouth.

Lockwood returned to the hotel, gathered his belongings, and carried them with him to the kitchen. When he pushed into the room, the hotel owner and his wife were having coffee at a wide wooden table. She saw Lockwood first. Her husband had to turn on the chair. He froze.

Lockwood put down his gatherings. The woman offered him coffee in a trembling voice. Her husband recognized the shell belt and holstered weapon from when he and the others had ransacked Lockwood's belongings. He edged toward the iron stove, white to the hairline. Lockwood ignored him, accepted the cup from his wife, and smiled as he thanked her.

The coffee was good. Maybe it really wasn't, but since Lockwood hadn't put anything in his stomach since morning, he thought it tasted good.

She had fried a steak, and the smell lingered. Lockwood put some silver atop the table for a meal. The woman shot her frightened husband a look and went about piling food on a plate. When Lockwood sat down and tipped his hat back, he smiled. The timid woman put a platter in front of him and smiled back. She then shot her husband a scorning look.

There was not a sound in the kitchen as Lockwood ate. The mousy woman refilled his coffee cup and asked if he liked the steak.

He looked up from eating. "As good as I've ever tasted," he told her and smiled again.

She sat down in the chair farthest from Lockwood. She could not get very close to the table. She looked a little disgusted at her petrified husband.

When Lockwood finished, he arose, put more silver beside the plate, got his gatherings in his left hand, and turned to leave. As he passed the stove, he swung, hard. The hotel keeper rolled along a drainboard near the stove before he collapsed. His wife had both hands over her mouth. Her eyes were enormous. She listened to Lockwood's bootsteps going toward the front door before she picked up a pitcher of water, upending it over her husband. When he choked, held up both arms to protect himself, and squawked at the woman, she put the pitcher aside, placed both hands on her hips, and said: "That man's no more a highwayman than I am! Get up and dry off!"

Lockwood went down to the livery barn where the sore-footed proprietor was sitting out front in the warm night, smoking a pipe that sounded like it had water in the bowl.

He leaned to knock out dottle as Lockwood came along. He grinned. "Nice town we got, ain't it? Marshal Duff was madder'n a hornet. Them damned fools."

Lockwood eased down beside the old man, put his gatherings on the ground, rolled a smoke, lighted it, and smiled. One thing bothered him. "He didn't say why he turned me loose. He just got rid of me an' said it'd be a good idea if I left town."

Alexander straightened around. "You didn't see him?"

"See who?"

"That damned highwayman. The marshal caught him when the thief's horse stepped in a hole and lamed up on him." Alexander was quiet for a moment then said what he had just figured out. "He must've left him with Doc O'Malley."

"The marshal shot him?"

"No. The way I heard it, when his horse stepped in the hole, he flung the highwayman over his head into some rocks. When the marshal come onto him, he was out cold an' bleedin' like a stuck hawg. The marshal brought him back tied across his lame horse. I got the horse out back. He's got an ankle as big as a small watermelon. Yep, that's about it. He left him to be patched up with Doc. I heard the danged fool had a gash on his head like he'd been damned near scalped."

Lockwood ground his smoke underfoot and arose. The livery man looked up. "You ain't leavin' in the night? Hell, if you paid up at the hotel, you'd better bed down in the hay until daylight."

Lockwood hesitated. The old man arose and jerked his head. "Come along. Ridin' at night's no way to travel."

Lockwood followed Alexander to a loft ladder, thanking the old man as he started climbing. The loft door, located at the far end of the barn in back, was hanging open. Enough light came through for Lockwood to find the highest mound of hay and burrow in. The next best aroma to a horseman, after horse sweat, was fragrant hay.

He slept like the dead. In the morning he awakened right at sunrise, pushed clear, stood up to pick hay off, heard someone below feeding stalled animals, and climbed down.

Alexander was bundled into a threadbare old coat. He did not see or hear Lockwood until he turned from forking his last flake of hay. He nodded. " 'Mornin'. You sleep good?"

Lockwood told the old man if folks filled mattresses with cured Timothy hay no one would awaken until after sunup.

The old man nodded in a bemused way. "Did you hear anythin' last night, Mister Lockwood?"

"I wouldn't have heard a cannon last night."

The old man shuffled to a bench and sat down. "Well, he got away last night."

Lockwood's eyes widened. "The highwayman?"

"Yep. I guess he played 'possum on Doc. Anyway, some time in the night he got away. When Doc's wife went to start the coffee boilin' this morning, he was gone." The old man raised unsmiling eyes. "An' the son of a bitch stole a horse off me." Alexander's unsmiling gaze lingered on Lockwood. "The marshal's on his trail. He run easterly. I didn't tell Marshal Duff. I expect he's a good lawman, but I don't like him an' never have."

"Didn't tell him what?"

"That horse he stole is cinch bound. Only thing I can figure is that when he saddled him, he didn't snug up the cinch." Alexander sat a moment in thought before he also said: "He's a damned good animal, dapple gray, tougher'n rawhide . . . but cinch bound. I expect, when the kid stops to rest and goes to snug up the cinch, Marshal Duff'll come onto him again. Maybe not hurt this time but afoot as sure as I'm settin' here."

Lockwood got his animal and had it rigged out ready to ride. He wanted to give the livery man some silver but couldn't find him.

Alexander was over at the cafe, one of the cafe man's first customers of the day. Nothing had changed for the old man in years — until the cafe man came from his cooking area to see who had opened and closed the door.

Alexander was speechless. At least until the shock passed, then he said, "What in hell happened to you?"

The cafe man waspishly asked what the livery man wanted for breakfast, took the order, and disappeared back into his cooking area. He knew for a fact he was going to be asked that question all day. If he told the truth, some if not all of his customers might not say it in front of him, but they would say it among themselves. He deserved what he had got.

Lockwood left Dunstan without haste and with an empty stomach. It wasn't the first time and wouldn't be the last. Somewhere along the trail he'd find food, particularly in a country which had ranches for most of the way back.

His horse was right up in the bit. He'd been rested, hayed, and grained, but most of all he was in his prime — seven years old and sound as new money. Lockwood let the reins swing. He had gone back. His heart still ached and most likely would as long as he lived when he thought of it.

If that's *all* she wanted of him, she would be satisfied. Most likely it meant a lot to her, and Lockwood certainly owed her that much. What he hadn't anticipated was her death at childbirth. When he left the barber shop after listening to what the barber back yonder had told him, he had sought the nearest bench. The shock had hit him like being kicked in the chest. Never once had he expected her to be dead, her parents gone out of the country, searching for a place where no one would know about their shame and their loss. Being young and thoughtless, he had ruined three lives.

He scarcely heeded the countryside until with a high hot sun overhead his horse picked up the gait a little and rode with pointed ears until they reached a creek where the horse would have drunk before the bridle could be removed if Lockwood had permitted it. He rode another couple of hours, until he saw a ranch yard southward a short distance and headed in that direction in search of a meal.

Chapter Sixteen

THE SHOCK OF A LIFETIME

The closer he got the more the buildings looked new. Instead of the log structures in the country he had come from, these buildings were of planed lumber, and they hadn't aged. There were the customary corrals behind the barn, the sheds for smithing, for wagon and buggy shelters, a bunkhouse with no smoke rising from the stove pipe. He only mildly wondered about that. It was not yet time for men to be preparing a meal.

He entered the yard in total silence, tied up out front of the barn, and stepped inside, expecting to find someone doing chores. What he saw was a sweat-stained, muscled-up dapple gray horse in a stall eating hay with the saddle still on him and the bridle draped from the saddlehorn.

He went to the half door and studied the horse. He'd been used hard, but as Alexander had said, he was tough as oak and as durable. The cinch was hanging loose under his belly. The horse scarcely acknowledged

Lockwood's presence. He was too intent on eating.

Lockwood returned to the yard. There was smoke rising over at the main house, although still none rising above the bunkhouse. Out back somewhere several horses nickered. It was past chore time, and they were hungry.

Lockwood crossed the yard, climbed the broad, wide steps, reached the door, and knocked. There was no response. The silence seemed to deepen. He could almost feel it.

He knocked again. This time a flush-faced man of middle years opened the door, stared, stepped aside for Lockwood to enter, then closed the door, and stood with his back to it.

For the second time in days Lockwood froze in place looking into a gun barrel, but this time it was a fully cocked six-gun. There were other people in the room. Two strapping young bucks and a large-boned, trim woman with a hint of gray. None of them moved or made a sound.

Lockwood wasn't surprised. He had guessed who had ridden that dapple gray into the yard. The man behind the gun was about Lockwood's height and build. His expression was tightly wound. He had no hat, just a crumpled bandage around his head above the eyes which showed blood.

Lockwood went to a chair, sank down, thumbed his hat back, and quietly said: "The law's after you. It's a wonder they haven't found this place. They've been out most of the night."

The injured outlaw had gray eyes set in a ruddy-complected face. He was young. He was also wild eyed. Lockwood's easy manner did not appear to have an effect upon the outlaw but made the rancher and his family slightly less tense.

The woman said: "Are you hungry?" to Lockwood and got an affirmative nod. But she made no move to go past the gunman to her kitchen. She simply stood there looking at him.

He finally addressed Lockwood. "Put the gun on the floor."

Lockwood obeyed slowly and carefully. When he straightened back, the gunman said: "Did you follow me here?"

"In the dark? No. Maybe that's what spoiled things for the marshal. But in another hour it'll be light enough."

The woman, who was obviously the mother of the pair of big, strong younger men who were roughly the same age as the outlaw, stared at the gunman as she said:

"Well? You got fed, what about him?"

The gunman did not take his eyes off Lockwood as he replied. "Make up a bundle of grub." He gestured with the gun for her to go to the kitchen.

The older man and the pair of strapping young ones watched the gunman. Lockwood did too; he was making a judgment. Of one thing he was fairly certain. The outlaw would shoot. He asked if the outlaw had the makings. Under the circumstances it was an almost incongruous thing to say. The outlaw shifted hands on his pistol, wiped sweat off his palms on the side of his britches, and did not answer Lockwood. Once, he shot a swift glance toward the front-wall window. It was getting steadily lighter. Dawn was arriving with sunlight right behind it. He snarled for the woman to move faster, then came out of his crouch slowly, leaned on the kitchen doorjamb, and considered the pair of large men about his own age. "I need a fresh horse."

Neither of them spoke, but their father did. He wanted the gunman out of his house any way he could accomplish it. "We got three stalled an' four in the corral. Take your pick an' go."

The gunman showed a thin, hard smile as he looked at the ruddy-complected man. "I will, an' the three of you'll go with me."

The woman came around into the parlor holding a bundle wrapped in a gingham tablecloth. She thrust it at the gunman. Lockwood had gauged the distance. It was too far. Even if the outlaw was diverted long enough to accept the bundle, Lockwood could still not reach him before he could pull the trigger.

The gunman told the woman to put the bundle by the door, which she did. As she straightened up, she looked steadily at the outlaw. She seemed to be waiting for something. Lockwood thought it might be riders from the bunkhouse. He had no way of knowing these people had no hired riders, that they ran their outfit by themselves. The bunkhouse had been something they had built against the day when they would have enough cattle to need extra hands.

The outlaw wig-wagged with his hand gun for the woman to get away from the door. She moved, still stiffly erect and silently defiant.

"You," the gunman said to Lockwood. "Pick up the bundle an' open the door. Good. Now then, all of us is goin' over to the barn while I saddle up. Go ahead. Lady, you lead."

They walked down across the yard with

the gunman in back. At the barn entrance he lined them up out front, sent one of the big young men to bring in the best horse they had, to switch his rigging to it and to be careful he didn't go out of his sight because, if he did, he was going to kill their parents.

The father nodded at one son. The other remained with his parents and Lockwood. The older man looked at his wife, raised his voice, and called to the man in the barn: "The runnin' mare, Mack."

They waited, with daylight getting brighter by the minute. When the gunman was peering down into the barn, Lockwood leaned over, palmed a stone, and hurled it across the yard. Fortune was with him. The stone struck a steel anvil strapped to a massive oak round. The sound was sudden and loud. The gunman swung instinctively. Lockwood launched himself. The gun went off when his shoulder hit the outlaw in the chest. Dirt spurted underfoot. Lockwood grabbed for cloth and pulled the outlaw in at the same moment he swung. The outlaw was fumbling with the hammer of his six-gun when the blow landed. He went over backwards, hit the ground hard, and Lockwood, putting his foot on the gun hand, leaned and wrenched away the weapon.

The ruddy-complected rancher and his

son rushed forward as the stunned outlaw rolled over to get purchase so he could arise, but he was too groggy. One of the rushing men hit him from the side. He rolled. There was a sound of tearing cloth and hard breathing. The woman grabbed a three-tined hay fork which was leaning nearby and went to help her husband and son.

Lockwood caught her, swung her around, took the fork from her, and snarled: "Get back out of the way."

She obeyed.

Her other son came running from inside the barn. He hesitated, watching the dazed outlaw trying to defend himself against his father and brother before also starting forward. Lockwood was standing as though he had taken root. Once, fleetingly, the struggling outlaw had rolled. His shirt in back was torn from neck to belt.

It was faint but recognizable, the birthmark on his back up high near the shoulder!

The shock immobilized Lockwood for moments during which the second son ran in swinging and cursing. His back was to Lockwood, who reached, spun the younger man, struck him alongside the jaw, and moved ahead before the body had stopped falling. The outlaw was being mercilessly beaten by the rancher and his son. He was trying to protect himself. He was no longer capable of fighting back.

Lockwood came in from the left side. As the ruddy-complected man leaned, knees sprung to strike, Lockwood caught him, swung, and pushed. The rancher went down in a heap. Before he could arise, Lockwood struck his other son under the ear. The man fell like a sack of wet grain across the outlaw. Lockwood pulled him off and helped the outlaw to get upright. His face was bleeding, so was his head wound. The bandage was soggy red. He could barely stand.

Lockwood picked up the outlaw's gun, dropped it into his holster, and pushed the dazed younger man into the barn where a leggy, fine-boned mare, sixteen hands if she was an inch, stood ready. Lockwood got his own horse snugged up, sprang across leather, and yelled for the dazed and battered outlaw to follow.

They burst out of the barn in a belly-down run, the outlaw with flapping reins, clinging to the saddle horn with both hands. The rancher and his wife were trying to tug one of their sons to his feet. They let go and sprang clear as the riders nearly ran over them. They stood like statues watching the strangers escape.

Lockwood edged close beside the Thoroughbred-looking tall mare in case the outlaw needed support. He didn't. He had a stranglehold on the horn, but he was still dazed. Instinct and nothing else kept him up there.

They ran the animals for a long mile before slackening off. The outlaw was a torn, bloody mess. His mind was clearing but, as they rode together, he only looked once at Lockwood.

The sun was high before Lockwood came to a creek, helped the outlaw down, led him to the water, and sluiced him down. Twice, while he was doing this, he looked impassively at the faint, uneven birthmark.

He rested longer than he thought was wise, but from here on his companion was going to have to have full command of himself. Somewhere behind them were irate cow people and very possibly that marshal from Dunstan with posse riders. The gingham-wrapped bundle of food was still in shade on the ground back by the barn. It would have come in handy now.

The outlaw went to the creek by himself, knelt, and splashed water. He also drank some. When he walked back, his stride was no longer unsteady.

They left the creek with a hot sun almost directly overhead. Neither of them had spoken a word yet, nor did they for another hour until they halted in a *bosque* of trees to re-bandage the outlaw's head. Strangely, the outlaw did not have a headache, which Lockwood said was a damned miracle. They had hit him with everything they had, and the wound had been torn open.

Lockwood retied it, a little tighter, and they left the trees with Lockwood sitting twisted, looking back. There was no sign of pursuit. He sat forward, hoping the marshal hadn't found the ranch before they had gotten ten miles on their way. He might find out someday why there was no pursuit but, if he did, too much time would have passed for it to matter.

Marshal Duffy with three possemen indeed reached the ranch yard about an hour after Lockwood and the outlaw had left it. Their horses were ridden down. The woman offered to feed them which Marshal Duffy gruffly declined and asked for the loan of fresh animals.

There were two stalled horses and one tied in the runway. His possemen took the pair of stalled horses. Marshal Duffy shifted his outfit to the tethered dapple gray. He moved swiftly to set the bridle, reaching under for the cinch as his two companions led their animals out front before mounting. Hurrying, Marshal Duffy looped the latigo twice, set back, and gave it a final, savage upward pull. The gray horse stood like stone, head up, utterly motionless.

Marshal Duffy did not want to waste even a moment. Instead of leading the gray horse out front, he twisted the stirrup, swung up, and sank his spurs. The men out front along with the ranch couple and their battered sons were looking inside the barn when it happened. The gray horse made a half squeal, half grunt and reared straight up. A horse on his hind legs was dangerous any time, but older horses lacked the flexibility of younger ones and very often lost their balance and fell backwards.

The gray was not an old horse. He was cinch bound. When Marshal Duffy had given that last savage pull on the latigo and swung up to hook the horse, he reared straight up and went over backwards. Men had been killed when an up-an-over, cinch-bound horse did that, usually because the saddle horn hit them squarely in the chest with all the animal's weight coming down on it.

Marshal Duffy had a second to realize what was happening and tried to throw himself sideways. He partially succeeded. The saddle horn came down with a thousand pounds atop it. If the barn runway hadn't been packed as hard as *caliche,* the horn would have been buried in the ground.

Marshal Duffy was pinned. Two men yelled as they ran into the barn. The horse rolled on its near side. Marshal Duffy was constrained by the stirrups on the off side. His leg was broken.

Later the spectators would shake their heads. If the rolling gray horse had toppled to the left instead of to the right, he would have fallen atop the lawman. The horse fought up to its feet, shaking and wild eyed. A posseman grabbed the bit to prevent the animal from breaking clear before the people on the other side could free Marshal Duffy's foot from the broken stirrup.

Afterwards there was to be no thought of pursuit. They carried the lawman to the house where the woman set and splintered the leg. Duffy alternated between consciousness and unconsciousness.

The sun began its westerly slide. Shadows appeared on the east side of trees, buildings, and deep arroyos. It also shaded creeks where willows lined the crooked course of water. Lockwood left the outlaw in the shade of a grassy creek bank and rode back a mile to top out on the rounded low knob of a fat hillock. There was no dust, no visible moving horsemen. The land lay serenely calm and empty as far as he could see.

As he rode back to the creek, he was thankful without wondering why that stubborn lawman had abandoned the pursuit. He hadn't struck Lockwood as the kind of individual who would be turned back even by the gates of hell.

He returned to the shaded creek, hobbled and off-saddled, cyed the sleeping, exhausted outlaw, and went to the water to wash, cool off, and roll a smoke from his diminished sack of tobacco. He should have been hungry, but the kind of stunning shock he had gotten back yonder during the fight left no room for hunger or, for that matter, much else beyond disbelief.

He sat, shaded by creek willows listening to the creek, lost in thought. He had not once asked anyone back there about the child. Not once. In fact it hadn't occurred to him after he had learned the mother had died in childbirth to dwell on anything but that soul-searing discovery.

He dropped the smoke into the water, arose, dusted off, and went back where their horses were still grazing. The younger man was still sleeping. Lockwood stood a long time looking down.

Chapter Seventeen

TIME TO MOVE ON

They needed food. Their animals required rest too, so the second day they did not push them. Lockwood was becoming convinced there was no pursuit or, if there was, it was too far behind to overtake them.

They left tracks; someone could be interested in that fact. At least someone should have been, but the farther they rode, with Lockwood occasionally seeking topouts from which to study their back-trail without finding any evidence they had pursuers, the more he came to accept the fact that for whatever reason they were not being pursued. That encouraged him to think about something to eat. The outlaw had been fed back yonder at the ranch house, but Lockwood hadn't.

They rarely spoke. The younger man might have. He looked terrible from his beating, but at least the bandage showed no fresh bleeding, and his eyes were clear. He had to be curious about Lockwood, about a man he had never seen before taking his part in that fight and who had afterwards made it possible for him to escape.

He wasn't surly by nature. He was taciturn, although at times a brooding silence made him seem surly. Since neither of them was particularly loquacious, Lockwood accepted the younger man's long periods of silence right up until the outlaw raised an arm pointing northward.

"See that cañon yonder with the trees in front?" He dropped his arm. "There's grub up there."

Lockwood silently turned northward, allowing his companion to take the lead. The trees and thorny brush at the cañon's mouth were almost impenetrable. The younger man picked up a faint, crooked trail which took them up a side hill through underbrush, then back down into the cañon, which broadened, became grassy, and had a piddling little warm-water creek running southward.

Lockwood was impressed. He'd never had reason to hide, but clearly his companion had. Not only did he have reason, but he had selected a place where only an experienced tracker could have found where the outlaw swung off and leaned to hobble his horse, his back to Lockwood. The older man also dismounted, stood with the hobbles in his hand, looking around. He saw no hide-out.

He knelt, buckled the hobbles, stood up, and off-saddled. The outlaw had already up-ended his saddle, draped the sweaty blanket wet side up, and was hanging the bridle from a young white oak when he said: "Home, sweet home." He turned, read Lockwood's expression, and shrugged. "It ain't all that far. Not when a man's got to range over a lot of country stayin' ahead of trouble."

Lockwood finished with his rigging, felt for the depleted Durham sack, and stood in pleasant shade rolling a smoke. After lighting up, he gazed at the younger man. "Did you rob that stage back in the Dunstan country?"

The youth gazed in the direction of an abrupt cañon wall held in place by a maze of thickets when he said: "Follow me" and, without showing any indication that he'd heard the question, went twisting and turning where the land rose slightly.

The cave was another epitome of seclusion. From its entrance Lockwood could see up and down the cañon and also across it where the horses were side by side, drinking at the creek. Inside, stony walls and a ceiling which would normally have been tan brown were nearly totally black from ancient smoke.

Lockwood sat near the opening. The cave was tall enough for men to stand erect and appeared to be fairly deep. The ground was powdery from dust that had known no moisture since God knew when. After his eyes became adjusted, he could make out primitive handiwork: huge bison, animals in flight he did not recognize, and a number of stick figures doing such things as pounding rocks in stone bowls, stretching wet hides, or just sitting.

The outlaw put two tins, one of peaches and the other of corn, in front of Lockwood, hunkered down opposite, and went to work with a small hatchet on one of the cans. When he had the hole he wanted, he tossed the hatchet to Lockwood, threw back his head to empty the tin of fruit of its juice, then lowered his head as he consumed the can's contents.

They ate in silence. Once or twice Lockwood looked out where the horses were swishing tails as they grazed still fairly close to each other. When he tossed his hat aside and leaned against a cool wall, he eyed his companion.

"You didn't answer about the stage," he said.

The younger man had a square, green tin from which he was dabbing caramel-colored ointment on his injuries. Food, rest, and safety made him less taciturn, but he still did not answer the question. Instead he asked one of his own.

"I thought you was the law. Why'd you take my side back there?"

Lockwood emptied the can of peaches before replying. It provided him time to think. "I didn't like the odds. They'd have beaten you to death."

"What's your name?"

"Cuff Lockwood. What's yours?"

"Jim Rider. It's not really my name. It's what folks call me behind my back. Only once did someone call me that to my face. I killed that son of a bitch. My real name is Jim Harrison. At least that was my maw's name. She died birthin' me." The youth raised his upper lip in a fierce smile, "I got no idea who my paw was. Some rider who was passin' through . . . that's all I know."

"So they called you Jim Rider?"

The youth nodded, clearly wishing this to end quickly. "Mister Lockwood, where you from?"

"A ranch some miles northeast of a place called Derby. It's another few days' ride from here. You ever hear of it?"

"I don't think so . . . maybe . . . but, if I did, I don't remember it. You live in Derby?"

"Not in Derby. We got a ranch upcountry from there."

"You got a family?"

"I got a wife," Lockwood replied and changed the subject. "Did you rob that stage north of Dunstan?"

"A man don't ask personal questions."

"You've been askin' 'em an' I been answerin' them."

The youth emptied his second tin, ran a filthy cuff from the torn shirt across his face, looking steadily at Lockwood. He finally said: "Yes, I robbed it. But someone else got the money box and the other stuff. I don't remember much . . . ridin' fast, duckin' an' dodgin', because I knew Duffy would be after me. He's another son of a bitch. That danged box was awkward to carry. That's about all I can remember. Duffy told me my horse lamed up in a squirrel hole." The youth made a sly smile. "I owe Duffy. He's another one who called me Jim Rider. Someday I'll settle up with him. He's a bullyin', mean son of a bitch. I wouldn't put it past him to keep the money box and other things for himself."

Lockwood knew hatred when he heard it. Marshal Duffy hadn't made a favorable impression on him, either, but that, he thought, was behind them both so he said: "You hang around the Dunstan country?"

"Yeah, I was born there. After they buried my maw, the old folks . . . the Harrisons, my maw's folks . . . sold out, left me with a washerwoman in town, and left the country."

"Where did they go?"

"I got no idea. By the time I was old enough to ask, there was a lot of new folks in the country. They didn't know. The older ones might have known, but they wouldn't have told me to save their lives."

Jim Rider made a death's head smile. "You asked, Mister Lockwood, an' I told you." The younger man unwound up from the ground, faded far back in the cave, and called from there. "A man never knows, does he?"

He returned wearing another shirt. It was clean but rumpled. It was also faded. He did a surprising thing. He pitched a sack of tobacco over to Lockwood. "I just naturally weasel things away. You never know, do you? I got a bottle of whiskey back there. . . ."

Lockwood shook his head as he thanked the youth for the tobacco which he pocketed without opening. He gazed down where the horses were dozing now, head to tail and swishing their tails to discourage those damned flies that entered a horse's nostrils, went into the belly, and laid eggs down there.

The youth was inspecting his injuries when Lockwood spoke without looking away from the horses. "Have you got other hide-outs?"

"Three. Miles from here in different places."

"As well stocked as this one?"

"Yes."

Lockwood did not ask thc obvious question — how had the youth managed to stock them? — but he did ask if the younger man had robbed other coaches.

"No. Just that one. I heard old Thompson at the store had a money box comin' from up north. I found out from a Messican yard-man at the corral yard which stage it would be on. I figured to go a long ways and start over with that money." The youth made his mirthless grin again. "I'll tell you for a fact I'll never try that again. I was lucky I didn't get shot. Two of the men inside . . . I made 'em empty their pockets. They both had loaded Derringers."

Lockwood smiled at the younger man's rueful expression. "Even the best ones don't last long, Jim. How'd you get by growin' up?"

"That woman the Harrisons left me with

. . . she was kindly, never hit me, but she worked the hell out of me."

"You were fond of her?"

"Yes. Especially when I was little, she'd tell me stories until I went to sleep. She . . . I never saw her drunk, but I never was close when she didn't smell of liquor. She was a widow woman."

The youth stopped talking, looked steadily at Lockwood, and asked another question. "How'd you happen to come to that ranch back yonder?"

"I was hungry."

The youth continued to regard Lockwood. "I seen you comin'. I told them folks not to make any noise. To let you in when you come to the house. I thought you'd be the law. I was real close to killin' you."

Lockwood finally broke the seal on the tobacco sack, rolled a smoke, and lighted it as he said: "I didn't figure you were. For one thing there was an empty chamber next to the one under the hammer. I figured there could be another empty casing under the hammer." Lockwood smiled a little. "But no man in his right mind would stake his life on that, would he?"

Jim Rider did not answer, nor did he say whether or not the cartridge casing under his hammer had a live charge. A full stomach and a sore body made him sleepy. He stretched out as he said: "We can stay here as long as we want. If anyone comes near, the horses'll let us know. You might as well rest, too, Mister Lockwood."

Lockwood went down to look at the horses. He didn't feel particularly tired. There were too many thoughts.

It was hot down in the cañon, hotter than it would be in open country. The horses were dozing in tree shade, no longer head to tail but with tails swishing. They knew he was there, but neither moved nor raised their ears.

A man would have had to be totally without conscience not to feel as Lockwood felt. There were no excuses, except the shallowest one, and there was no way to place blame anywhere else.

He knelt at the warm-water creek, drank, washed, and sat in the grass until gnats drove him away. He felt something now he had never felt before — old.

A fat marmot emerged from his hole in jerky little stops and starts. His eyes were weak, but there was nothing wrong with his nose, which he twitched as he came more than half way from the hole testing, sniffing, analyzing, speculating in his marmot's mind.

He had claws capable of tearing flesh.

Lockwood sat perfectly still, watching. The hairy creature finally left his hole, going toward the creek where he alternately drank and flung up his head. Lockwood idly thought it must be difficult to spend a whole lifetime being afraid, having to be constantly on guard.

The marmot half raised himself, wriggled his nose faster, paused for seconds facing in Lockwood's direction, then fled faster than Lockwood thought he could, and whipped out of sight into his hole. He had caught the most dreaded scent of all, man scent.

The heat worked on Lockwood, as did the sound of the creek. He lay back with his hat over his face and slept. When he awakened, it was dark. There was no moon, not directly overhead anyway, but the identical pattern of stars was up there.

He returned to the hide-out, smelled cooking before he had completed the trip, and moved inside the cave where the younger man was making supper near enough the cave's opening for most of the smoke to go outward, but there was very little smoke. Jim Rider was burning dry sticks.

He squinted up at Lockwood. "Anything wrong?"

Lockwood sank down, shaking his head. "No. What're you cooking?"

"I ain't sure. I stole it off a bench some farm woman had set jars out on. It think it's beef. It smells like it."

Lockwood had visions of a youngster learning to steal early, getting better at it because he didn't want to starve, and feeling no guilt about it. The way Jim Rider had answered, Lockwood knew Jim Rider'd developed a lack of conscience about doing whatever was necessary to keep body and soul together.

It was indeed beef. They had a good supper. Lockwood missed coffee, but there was none. Otherwise it was an excellent meal.

When they were cleaning their tin plates, Jim Rider said: "I come here when I can. It's like a home to me. Private, pleasant, real restful." He grinned at Lockwood. "Everyone's got to have a home, don't they?"

Lockwood nodded without speaking.

They sat like Indians, quiet, replete, gazing into the dying little dry-wood fire. Occasionally Lockwood gazed across the fire. Jim Rider had grown up resourceful, independent, and tough. He eventually stretched out to sleep, thinking Jim Rider probably had precious few good memories, and that troubled him too.

The following morning Lockwood found cougar tracks at the creek. There must have been a breeze blowing the wrong way last night or their horses would have made a racket. There were three things all horses feared, even ones that had never lived in unsettled country: cougars, bears, and wolves. Of those three they feared big cats the most. The other two were usually noisy and, given sufficient warning, could be outrun, but cougars were soundless. By the time they were in position to attack, it was too late to run.

When he got back to the hide-out where Jim was making breakfast, he mentioned the mountain lion. Jim Rider nodded without noticeable concern. "It's wild country, Mister Lockwood. Sure wish we had coffee."

After their first meal of the day Jim Rider went down to the creek for a bath. Lockwood found a narrow game trail, followed it to the countryside above, and made a careful study of the land as far as he could see. Not until he was ready to go back down the trail did faint, distant movement catch his attention. Whoever, or whatever it was, looked to be a hell of a distance away and northwesterly.

Lockwood squatted to watch. There was dust, almost invisible at that distance, but the longer he watched, the more visible it became. Whatever made that dust was moving right along. He thought it was a rider, perhaps two riders. Yet the longer he watched, the more it did not seem to be a pair of riders, but rather something wider and thicker, like possibly a light wagon.

Jim Rider came up out of the cañon, saw the dust banner, and squatted beside Lockwood without saying a word for a long time.

Lockwood asked him if he could make out the moving object. Rider shook his head before speaking. "I got no idea, but it's comin' from the direction of the Dunstan country." He thought briefly then spoke again. "He's too far north to be followin' our tracks."

Lockwood had already reached that conclusion. As they hunkered there, the younger man, presumably with the perfect vision of youth, said: "It's a top buggy." He sounded surprised. "What the hell's a top buggy doin' out here? There ain't a town within miles. An old ranch couple miles north is all."

Lockwood's retort was crisp. "Got to be a ranch. There's cattle."

They squatted and watched until they could clearly make out a top buggy being pulled by a large, powerful horse with a big stud neck. It held steadily to a course directly toward the watching men.

Lockwood was wary, but the man beside him looked clearly puzzled. "The nearest ranch yard, as far as I know anyway, is northeast about two, three miles. He's got to veer off northward soon."

Lockwood sighed. "Who knows about your hide-out, Jim?"

"As far as I know, don't no one know about it. Hell, it's a woman!"

The rig came ahead at a slogging trot. The powerful animal between the shafts was sweat shiny. Lockwood and his companion dropped down below the cañon wall with just their heads and shoulders showing. The rig was finally close enough for them to see the driver, and it really was a woman.

She slackened off about a half mile from the cañon, let the horse walk, and leaned from beneath the buggy top as though watching for something. Lockwood and Jim Rider scarcely breathed as the rig approached within a hundred yards of their hiding place, abruptly turned north, and skirted along the top of the cañon.

They crept out and watched, still from hiding. The rig halted a fair distance northward. The woman leaned out and shouted.

"Sonny! Sonny you come up here right this instant!"

For some minutes nothing happened. Not

until the woman climbed down from the buggy, took the whip from its socket, and marched angrily closer to the cañon's rim where she halted, hands on hips, and shouted again. "You come over here right this instant. Paw's goin' to tan your britches. I know you're in there. *Right now!*"

Lockwood was fascinated. It was as though neither he nor his companion existed. A gangling boy stood up out of a thicket, looking more sheepish than afraid. The woman berated him and waved the buggy whip. The lad emerged from his hiding place with an old flintlock musket. He tried to talk, but the woman's anger was overwhelming. She gave him a cut along the back of his legs as he went around to the off side and climbed into the rig.

He was still trying to get words in edgewise when the woman climbed in, rammed the whip into its dashboard socket, and turned the horse back the way she had come. Finally, the boy was able to speak. "I had enough grub for three days, sis. Besides, Paw told me I could take the old gun an' go huntin'."

"He didn't mean you could walk this far. You give the whole family fits when you didn't come home last night."

"Sis . . . ?"

"Sonny, I just don't know what we're goin' to do with you."

"Sis . . . ?"

"Don't you 'sis' me!"

"Sis. There's two men livin' down in that cañon. I seen their horses. I seen them too. One's got a rag around his head."

She faced the boy with an expression of horror. "Renegades! Sonny, they might have killed you. Outlaws hidin' out. We'll tell Paw."

Lockwood faced his companion. "Time to move on," he said.

They went back down the trail where their horses were contentedly grazing side by side.

Chapter Eighteen

GUNS!

They looked like a pair of resurrected corpses, filthy, ragged, unwashed, stained. If the father of that lad back yonder had come back with riders, it would have been hard to convince them they weren't outlaws.

Because the horses were fresh, they made excellent mileage on this particular day. Lockwood saw the dome-topped wagon with its stove pipe sticking through the roof. Jim saw it too and looked puzzled until they were close enough to see sheep, but before they got much closer several dogs began raising hell.

Lockwood saw the shepherd come from in front of his wagon, stop and watch them for a while, before ducking inside his wagon and emerging with a Winchester rifle. Lockwood told his companion to raise his right hand. They both offered that age-old signal of men approaching in peace.

The shepherd stepped over into wagon shade, called to his dogs in a language Jim Rider scowled about, and the dogs stopped barking. The sheep herder recognized Lockwood but faintly frowned as both riders came up and swung off. The Basque's gaze lingered longest on the younger man with the bandaged head and bruised, swollen face.

Lockwood made motions like someone eating and smiled. The shepherd straightened up slowly, went inside his wagon, and when he emerged this time, he had left the rifle behind. He had two tin dishes heaped with what looked like large fat worms covered with some kind of peppery gravy. Hungry men were not choosy. They squatted in the shade of their horses and ate. The wormlike things were not dissimilar to chicken necks. They had to be eaten with the fingers and had a wonderful taste. The sheep herder brought them half a torn loaf of round bread for sopping up the gravy.

Not a word was passed until the riders were ready to hand back the tin plates, then Lockwood, remembering his earlier visit, made elaborate gestures about drinking water. This time the shepherd returned with a large bottle encased in burlap. It was red wine. All three men drank before the sheep herder placed the jug beneath the wagon where it would stay cool and pointed to Jim Rider's bandaged head. He said something which was totally incomprehensible, then made his own variety of hand gestures to indicate washing and re-bandaging Jim's head.

Lockwood told his companion to sit on a small keg. He had a little difficulty removing the bandage. It appeared to be stuck to the youth's head. The Basque stopped Lockwood and came forward with a canteen. He soaked the cloth, worked it loose without opening the wound, then ducked back into his wagon and reappeared with a dented old tin from which he smeared Rider's head with something that smelled slightly rancid. It was lanolin. A hundred years in the future people would not have improved on its healing ability.

He made a fresh bandage, much smaller this time, then stood back inspecting his handiwork. Lockwood said: "Good. Very good," and the Basque smiled broadly. He went under the wagon and returned with the sack-wrapped bottle. All three of them drank again. The Basque was replacing the bottle when someone called from a fair distance. The shepherd sprang back upright. There were four riders approaching at a walk.

Lockwood and Jim Rider studied the strangers. They were stockmen, which was no surprise, and each man had a carbine slung forward in the boot under his *rosadero*. They rode bunched up and unsmiling.

The shepherd said something and turned to go inside his wagon. One of the approaching men aimed and fired. The sound echoed after wood splintered beside the sheep herder. He jumped back and turned, facing the riders. Lockwood had a six-gun. Jim had an empty holster.

The strangers stopped about seventy-five feet from the wagon and sat in silence. They were hard-looking, faded, weathered rangemen. Two had beards; the other two had beard shadow.

The oldest among them, the same man who had fired that warning shot, leaned aside to expectorate amber-colored saliva, straightened up, and jutted his jaw at Lockwood. "Who're you? What're you doin' here?"

Lockwood answered quietly. "We was passin' through. Who are you?"

The older man leaned on his saddle horn, studying Lockwood. "It ain't none of your business, but I'll tell you. I'm Jack Garth. These gents ride with me."

"You own this range, Mister Garth?" Lockwood asked.

"We're grazin' through, cowboy, an' we don't like sheep."

Lockwood nodded. They were free-grazers, the kind of men established rangemen loathed with a passion. Free-grazers bought thin cattle and started driving them over unfenced land, kept on eating off other people's grass until autumn, then headed for a railroad shipping yard and sold their beef. They owned nothing except maybe a trail wagon, their outfits, and some horses.

Lockwood said: "Free-grazers, Mister Garth?"

The hard, unkempt, older man fixed Lockwood with a challenging look as he said: "Does that bother you, mister?"

Lockwood ignored the question. "This sheepman's got as much right here as you have."

The older man straightened back slowly. His three younger companions did not take their eyes off Lockwood. They had already noticed that bandage-headed youth with Lockwood had an empty holster.

The older man leaned forward to dismount as he spoke to his companions. "Fetch the can of coal oil."

He was on the ground when Lockwood drew and cocked his Colt. All three free-grazers froze. The older man eyed Lockwood through a thoughtful moment before speaking. "Don't get in the way, mister.

We're goin' to burn the wagon and run off the sheep. Are you a cowman?"

Lockwood did not answer this question either. Instead he tipped his gun barrel until it was centered on the older man's chest. "Get back in the saddle," he said quietly.

The free-grazer studied Lockwood for a moment then turned to toe into the stirrup. His left hand was on the saddle horn when he suddenly twisted, drew, and fired.

Lockwood let the hammer fall before he himself fell. The free-grazer's horse sprang violently sideways. It struck the nearest horse hard enough to knock it against another horse. The first man managed to stay up there, but the second free-grazer went off sideways.

The only unaffected free-grazer was too startled by what had happened to reach for his holster. When he finally made the move, Lockwood fired from the ground. The horseman seemed to have been struck by an invisible fist. He dropped both reins, went so far backwards he cleared the cantle, and fell. His terrified mount whirled, stepped squarely on the man's chest, and fled.

Jim Rider dove for the gun the older free-grazer had dropped, grabbed it, and aimed at the man on the ground, but that free-grazer had been stunned by his fall and barely more than pushed himself up into a sitting position. Jim Rider did not fire.

The remaining free-grazer whirled, sunk in his hooks, and fled southward, riding like the wind, hunched too low to be a target. He dropped a container which shattered on the ground, spilling coal oil in all directions.

Jim had a prisoner. He punched the man to his feet and pushed the cocked six-gun into the man's soft parts. He said: "Walk, you son of a bitch. Keep walkin' an', if you so much as turn your head, I'll kill you. *Start walking!*"

The remaining free-grazer walked southward. He did not once look back. Jim scooped up the gun which had fallen from the man's holster, leathered it, and turned.

The shepherd was working frantically. He was on his knees beside Lockwood, who was attempting to prop himself up with one arm. The Basque pushed him gently to the ground.

Jim went over to stand like a rock. Lockwood was bleeding. His shirt was scarlet and limp. The shepherd sprang up, ran to his wagon, and ran back with a stick and a thong of rawhide which he fashioned around Lockwood's upper arm, twisting slowly until the bleeding stopped. He looked up at Jim and gestured for him to hold the stick. He ran back to his wagon.

The free-grazer's bullet had hit Lockwood between his upper right side and his arm. The side wound bled but not as fiercely as the arm wound. Two of the free-grazers' horses only went as far as where the hobbled horses were grazing along with the big, feather-legged wagon animals. The Basque brought a chipped, old, enameled basin half full of water and a small blue bottle. He cut away the sleeve and shook the blue bottle as he said something to Lockwood. He might as well have been trying to explain something to a rock.

He unstoppered the little bottle, got as close as he could, and poured a bluish liquid into the wounds. Lockwood almost sprang to his feet before he fainted.

The sheep herder spoke rapidly to Jim Rider, trying to explain what he had done. The youth watched Lockwood and ignored the Basque, who now used clean rags to cleanse thoroughly the bloodless wounds and bandage them. The arm wound presented no problems, but the rib-cage wound did. The Basque did the best he could and sat back on his heels, looking at the unconscious man.

The sheep herder took back the stick with its twisted rawhide and very slowly released it a turn at a time. The bleeding started. The Basque sat down to be more comfortable and took his time about unwinding the rawhide.

Jim Rider went over to the dead men, took their weapons, rolled them both face down, went out where the horses were grazing, dumped the riding gear of the dead men, and did not use the hobbles attached to each saddle. When he returned, the shepherd was still loosening the thong a fraction at a time. He looked up at Jim and shrugged.

Time passed; shadows thickened; Jim started a little fire. The Basque brought an old blanket from his wagon to spread over Lockwood. He got Jim to prop Lockwood up while he trickled red wine into him.

Lockwood choked, coughed, spat, and opened his eyes. His arm felt like it was burning. His side also hurt but not as much. He tried to look at his wounds but couldn't. He saw Jim supporting him and asked: "What happened? I got shot?"

"The sheep herder poured some bluish looking liquid on your wounds an' you passed out."

The Basque took three or four swallows from the sacking-wrapped bottle and offered it to Jim, who shook his head. He then held it toward Lockwood, and the wounded man leaned forward. This time he needed less support, and he drank more than they had been able to trickle down him before.

Jim rolled a saddle blanket for a pillow and placed it under Lockwood's head. He then returned to feed the fire and squatted there, solemn as an owl.

Eventually, when the Basque could loosen the thong without encouraging more bleeding, he set the tourniquet and joined Jim Rider at the fire. He brought food from his wagon, several old iron pans, and went to work wordlessly preparing a meal. From time to time he would glance over at the man under the blanket.

He also glanced at the wounded man's companion from time to time. Jim Rider was like a carving. He neither moved nor seemed aware of what was happening around him.

Lockwood would not eat, but he drank quite a bit of the red wine. The last time Jim went to look at him Lockwood was asleep.

Jim helped the Basque bring in his sheep. He had no corral. He didn't need one; his dogs were better; if a coyote got too close, they ganged up and killed it.

In the morning Lockwood's side and arm were badly discolored and swollen. Jim squatted and fumed. Lockwood needed a doctor. As far as he knew, there wasn't a town, much less a doctor, within a hundred miles. He was in country he did not know at all.

He thought of commandeering the shepherd's team and wagon to take Lockwood to whichever town he came to first. He could have done it. He was armed. The Basque was not.

He sat gazing at the sleeping man knowing very well that, if Lockwood could have spoken to him, he would have told Jim doing something like that to a man who had helped them was bad. He and Lockwood had come to know each other very well since Dunstan. There was nothing to do but stay put until Lockwood could ride.

It required a full week and even then, although Lockwood seemed capable enough, Jim had to lift him into the saddle. The Basque watched, shook his head, and remained silent right up until Lockwood leaned from the saddle with gold coins in his hand. The sheep herder shook his head violently, made some kind of protest in his own language, and stepped back. Lockwood leaned, dropped the coins, reined around, and rode away.

They did not look back. The sun was warm. The sky was clear. Distances seemed to dance a little as heat arrived. Jim asked Lockwood several times how he felt. The answer was always the same.

"A hell of a lot better'n I look. Do you know what that medicine was he used back yonder? Ground blue vitriol mixed with oil. There's nothing in this world that I know of anyway that hurts like that stuff in an open wound."

"Does it do any good?"

"I've used it on horses since before you were born. I know it burns like hell, but they never get proud flesh, and their wounds heal clean."

"He was a real decent feller . . . wherever he came from."

Lockwood agreed. "I thought he was Spanish or Mex, but I've heard folks speak Spanish and, whatever that feller spoke, it sure wasn't Spanish."

Lockwood was drooping by mid-afternoon. Jim watched for water and firewood before setting up camp. He wished he had some of that red wine. The best he could do was keep the fire going all night and make certain Lockwood didn't get chilled. It was all he knew to do.

In the morning Jim heated some of those fat worms in that pepper gravy the Basque had given him. It would have gone down better with coffee, but they had none.

Later, when Jim was rigging out both horses, Lockwood asked if he had liked that pepper gravy and meat. Jim nodded and Lockwood said: "That was lambs' tails." At the look he got from Jim Rider, he smiled. "Didn't you notice none of the lambs had long tails?"

Jim hadn't noticed for the best of all reasons. He knew absolutely nothing about sheep and cared less.

"That's how they keep tally. Each time they dock a tail, they drop it in a bucket. At the end of the day they count tails and that's how many sheep they worked that day."

"That's what we ate?"

"Yeah. There's not much meat on a tail. A man's got to eat a lot of them, but it was good, wasn't it?"

Jim side-stepped an answer by asking his own question. "Do you run sheep?"

"No. Cattle. But when I was growing up, I worked for folks who had woollies."

Lockwood was back in familiar country. As he rode, he wondered whether it might not be a good idea to go down to Derby, get cleaned up, and put on some decent clothes before heading for the ranch.

They had Derby in sight before he decided to go directly home. For one thing his wounds were troublesome. The swelling was uncomfortable. For another thing if he arrived in Derby looking the way he looked, with a younger rider at his side who looked just as bad, maybe worse, it would encourage questions which he did not want to answer, not now, maybe not ever.

Chapter Nineteen

LOCKWOOD'S RETURN

The arm was troublesome, but the wound in the side felt feverish and was beginning to send flashes of intense pain. When the swollen arm touched the side wound, those spasms of pain were almost more than a man could bear. Nor did it help that the Basque, wise though he had seemed to have been about such things, had only very slowly released the tourniquet thong, allowing blood to circulate inadequately and very slowly. The result was a mildly painful tingling sensation which would diminish in time but hadn't up until now.

Lockwood began edging away from rooftops when he and his companion had Derby in sight, which brought a quick comment from Jim Rider.

"They might have a doctor down yonder, an' you sure need one, Mister Lockwood."

There was no question about Lockwood's needing a doctor, but he had been gone a long time. He missed his wife, the riders, especially Evan Turlock, even Francesca, so he held to the course leading away from Derby.

The sun was high and hot before Lockwood saw the unkempt old trees, then the large log barn, and finally the main house.

He smiled at the younger man. "Home."

Jim slouched along, studying the large yard ahead, the buildings, the old trees. He could not avoid the feeling of permanence, of order and success. He asked if maybe it might not be better if they split up here.

Lockwood looked around. "I have plans for you," he told the youth. "We need another rider."

"I don't know anythin' about cowboyin', Mister Lockwood."

"You can learn. Jim, a man should have a trade. One of the fellers up ahead . . . Evan Turlock . . . is as good man as you'll ever meet. He knows the business inside and out, an' he's got all the patience in the world."

Jim broodingly watched the buildings get closer. "Mister Lockwood, I ain't sure I want to learn cowboyin'."

For almost a quarter mile Lockwood rode beside the youth without speaking or looking away from him. During his quiet times on the ride back he had imagined the youth working on the ranch, settling in, learning things foot-loose, novice outlaws needed to know, like responsibility, self-discipline, a working trade.

They were less than a half mile from the yard when Jim reined up, dropped both hands to the saddle horn, and sat looking solemnly ahead. "Mister Lockwood . . . ?"

The pain in the side came on suddenly, so sharply Lockwood leaned forward, locking his jaws against making a sound. It was almost as sharp and overpowering as the blue vitriol had been. Sweat burst out. He gripped the reins until his knuckles were white.

"Mister Lockwood? You all right? I'll help you down."

Most abrupt pains either vanished as suddenly as they had arrived or at least lessened. This one didn't. Lockwood leaned so the youth could take the weight as he eased the older man to the ground. Lockwood was sweat slippery. His face was gray. He could not distinguish the youth clearly.

He tried to keep his breathing steady and failed. Jim knelt beside him, bewildered and frightened. "I'll get help," he said finally.

Leaving Lockwood lying in the grass, he sprang a-horseback and raced into the yard, yelling. A heavy, dark woman appeared on the porch. He saw her, slid to a halt, crowding words together and twisting to point back where a horse was standing over a man on the ground.

Francesca was as shocked by the youth's appearance, filthy, stubbled, as she was by what he was saying. A second woman appeared, taller, spare, with a rock set to her jaw and steely blue eyes. The youth repeated what he had told the heavier woman.

There was a faint spindrift of smoke arising above the bunkhouse, but no one appeared for a good reason. Evan and the riders had been gone since early morning.

The erect, steely-eyed woman looked out where the horse was patiently trailing reins in the grass and turned. "I'll hitch the wagon. Francesca, get some blankets." She faced the agitated youth. "Help me with the wagon."

Jim swung off, looped reins over the tie rack, and had to lengthen his stride to keep up with the tall woman. He pulled the wagon out as she went for the team. It was slow work, but they moved as fast as they could. By the time they were ready to leave the yard, Francesca had brought blankets and, after hesitating a moment, eased up into the wagon bed and held on.

The distance was not great, but Toby Lockwood urged the team anyway. The youth beside her spoke, got no answer, and looked at her profile. Her lips were sucked flat. Her forehead had a faint crease across it, and her bearing was of someone who was not interested in talking.

To those who had known her over the years, she would have been instantly recognizable as the Lady Barlow of former times. The iron woman of resolve and initiative. When they wheeled in close to the man in the grass, Jim sprang down, kneeling with his back to the woman so he did not see the congealed looks of recognition and horror.

Then Jim twisted to look back. "He's unconscious. He's sweatin' like I never seen anyone sweat before."

The women alighted. Toby looked at her husband, jerked her head, and told the youth to let down the tailgate. While he was doing this, Francesca rolled her eyes upward and crossed herself, then met the gaze of Lockwood's wife and said: "He looks terrible."

Toby ignored that. She gestured for the others to help lift Lockwood. They eased him into the bed of the wagon and, while the youth and Francesca were arranging the blankets, Toby climbed up, loosened the binders, and headed for the yard, her expression like granite and the same color.

They carried Lockwood inside, took him to the same room he'd been put in that other time when he'd been very ill, and Toby gave more orders. "Boy, take care of the wagon an' the horses. Francesca, some hot beef broth with a dram in it. He's filthy."

Francesca spoke from the doorway. "It looks like a bad wound."

Toby was peeling away Lockwood's clothing. She began with his boots. She put the filthy clothing in a heap, rolled up her sleeves, and went to the kitchen to fill a large pan with hot water into which she tossed a cloth along with a bar of soap.

Francesca said: "I think he needs the doctor."

Toby nodded and, without speaking, carried the heavy pan of water back to the bedroom. Her hair was working loose; several strands fell across her forehead. She ignored them and everything else as she peeled off the Basque's bandages, using hot water to loosen them, leaned down close to examine the wounds, and only straightened up when Francesca arrived with the broth.

Francesca blanched at sight of the bared wounds. "There is that new doctor down in Derby," she quietly said, staring at the swollen, discolored flesh.

Toby did not answer. She scrubbed Lockwood as though her mind was closed to all else. The only part of him she was gentle with was his injured rib-cage and the arm.

They got a little hot broth down him. His throat closed after several swallows, and Francesca left the room praying under her breath. At that moment, while she was not a gambling person — her faith prohibited it — if she had been, she would have wagered all she owned that Lockwood was going to die.

Jim returned to the house. He had washed and combed his hair, which was only a marginal improvement. Toby sat him in a chair, examining his bruises and his wound. Francesca stood nearby, hands clasped beneath her apron. This one she would not have wagered on, although the clear signs of a bad beating along with the head wound did not incline her to believe he would be normal for a long time. Francesca had forgotten how quickly the young recover.

Toby asked questions of Jim as she worked on him. His answers for the most part were curt and cryptic. He had not been around many women, and the ones he had been around had not been like this woman. He told them about the sheep herder, which was where Lockwood had been wounded. He also told them about the trouble back in Dunstan, but in both cases imparted only a minimum of information.

When Toby finished, she told him to go to the bunkhouse and stake out a bunk. Francesca waited until he had closed the door then said: "But he didn't say where he met your husband."

Toby nodded. She had formed an opinion which was partially correct. The youth was not very talkative. It did not occur to her she was the reason.

Lockwood was feverish when Toby brought a lamp to his room after supper. She used a cool cloth to wipe his face. From the doorway Francesca repeated the statement about the new doctor down in Derby, only this time she added a little more.

"I know ways to lower a fever, but what he needs is something more than a *curandera.* I wouldn't wait." Toby turned, and Francesca made her final comment. "This way he will get worse. Maybe with the doctor it will also happen. At least let me send for him. He cannot make your husband die any sooner, can he?"

Toby followed Francesca to the kitchen where she dropped down on a chair with a cup of black coffee. "See if Evan is back. If he is, ask him to find the doctor and bring him back."

Francesca left the house while Toby Lockwood continued holding the cup and staring at the wall.

When the heavy, dark woman returned, she too sat down at the table. "Evan is going. He's going to take the boy with him."

Toby raised questioning eyes.

Francesca shrugged. "He wanted to go. He said he could tell the doctor what had happened, how suddenly your husband got sick."

Toby took a lamp and tip-toed into the bedroom. Lockwood watched until she had put the lamp down then spoke in a tired-sounding tone of voice. "It come on sudden, but hours before we got near, I had a sort of burnin', hot feeling."

Toby sat down at bedside, expressionless except around the eyes. "The lad told me what happened at the sheep camp. Cuff, you should have ridden to Derby. There's a medical doctor down there now."

His eyes showed an ironic twinkle when he answered. "There's a lot of things I should have done, Toby. You look mighty good to me."

Her voice was softly unsteady when she replied. "You look good to me, Cuff."

"But you've seen me look better?"

She smiled. "Evan's gone for the doctor."

"You already said that."

"You were filthy. I bathed you. Cuff, that arm doesn't look very good."

He made a weak effort to lift the arm, desisted because of pain, and raised his gaze to the ceiling, the same ceiling he'd seen over many years. It was good to be home in bed.

"Are you hungry?"

"No, but I'm thirsty."

She left the room. Lockwood saw the pile of soiled clothes, rolled his head in the other direction and gazed at the portrait of his wife beside the big old dresser. She was dressed as he had first seen her, right down to the braided quirt hanging from a wrist. He had always liked that portrait.

She returned, watched as he emptied the glass, and got a big-eyed expression as she took the empty glass. "Francesca's idea. She said whiskey in water is good for the heart and blood."

He grinned. "On an empty stomach I can tell you it's right enlivenin'." Five minutes later he was asleep.

Francesca had told her it would do that too. She left the room. The men at the bunkhouse had heard from the youthful stranger about their boss. One of them, a tousle-headed man, came hat in hand to the front door to make enquiries. Toby reassured him. He carried that back to the others. They drank a toast to Lockwood's recovery, which was the best excuse they'd had in months for having an after-supper drink.

When the physician arrived, Toby got a shock. He was dark. She thought he was Mexican, but the features were not right for that. Without further speculation she led him to Lockwood's room and turned up the lamp. He asked if she had another lamp. After she had left the room, the physician talked to Lockwood as he examined him. By the time Toby returned and the room was brighter, the physician ignored her, sat down facing the bed, and asked more questions.

Lockwood answered them. The whiskey was still working. He even smiled when he told the doctor about two women and a boy carrying him inside and putting him to bed. "I never been that helpless before in my life."

The doctor's dark eyes brightened with understanding. He then made a remark that startled Toby and to some degree did the same to her husband. He said: "My name is Alfred Smith. My real name is Tenkiller." The physician smiled. "When I enrolled in medical college, the admissions woman suggested Smith, Alfred for her father, Smith for her maiden name. She was likable. So . . . here sits beside you

Doctor Alfred Smith . . . Tenkiller."

At the long silence his remarks had caused, the physician relaxed, crossed his legs, and looked at them both. "Northern Cheyenne. Mister Lockwood, I never learned how to scalp people . . . but while I was in college, believe me, if I had known, there were some I would have liked to scalp." Doctor Smith considered Lockwood before continuing. "I'll tell you what you have. Very bad inflammation and the beginning of an infection that could spread and kill you."

Toby sat erect. Lockwood's eyes did not leave the physician's face. Doctor Smith let the silence linger before saying, "For bad cases of infection, which usually become blood poisoning, there is little to be done. In your case . . . are those the clothes you were wearing?"

Lockwood nodded.

"Filthy. Mister Lockwood, that's how you get blood poisoning, dirty clothing and dirty body."

Toby interrupted. "You can't let him die!"

The dark eyes swung to her. "I'm not going to let him die . . . but all my training, all the knowledge I acquired, says once blood poisoning starts, people die. Some quicker than others, but they die."

The doctor shifted on his chair, glanced briefly at the little leather satchel he had set aside before examining Lockwood. He turned back to face Lockwood. "Any physician, you see, will tell you that blood poisoning kills." Dr. Smith looked steadily at Lockwood. "I have medication in that bag. It's supposed to slow the spread. It doesn't do any such thing. Mister Lockwood," he paused again. "I could tell you how they almost dismissed me from medical college when I told them blood poisoning can be cured. The Cheyenne and Sioux have been curing infections for more years than anyone knows. They scorned me. Now . . . it is up to you. Their medicine, the same that I learned and practice, will not prevent you from dying if your infection spreads. Maybe my medicine won't either, but I know that it has stopped the spread. It has kept people from dying. Mister Lockwood?"

Only the very faint sound of burning wicks in the lamps were audible in the room. Toby looked at her husband. She had already reached a decision, but it was Lockwood's choice.

She leaned over, took his hand, and tightened her fingers. Lockwood said: "Not much of a choice, is it?"

The physician answered shortly. "I think

it's a very good choice. But only if you act fast."

Lockwood weakly nodded. "Any time you're ready, Doctor."

The physician went to his little satchel as he told Toby he would need a glass of water. After she departed, the doctor smiled at Lockwood and imitated a blanket Indian. "I bet many horses you walk again."

Lockwood grinned. "If you're right, you can have many horses."

When Toby returned, the physician tapped some gray powder from a small bottle into the water, shook it as he approached the bed, and said: "Drink it."

As Lockwood was drinking, the physician returned to the satchel, handed Toby the small bottle with instructions. "Twice a day until the powder is gone. That should take four days. I'll come back on the fifth day." He snapped the satchel closed and stood gazing toward the bed. "Remember, many horses, Mister Lockwood."

After the doctor departed, Toby held the small bottle to a lamp and said: "It looks like grayish dirt."

Lockwood said nothing. He had belched after drinking; the taste in his mouth was somewhere between mummified earth and rotten weeds.

He slept the night away and would have continued sleeping if Toby hadn't appeared with another glass of medicine. Lockwood drank it and grimaced. Toby did not smile. He said: "I'd marry you for some breakfast."

That time she smiled.

Later, Jim came to see Lockwood. They talked of the only things they had in common, their shared experiences. When he arose to depart, Jim said: "You were right about Evan. I'm goin' out with him an' the others. Maybe I'll see you when we get back."

Lockwood slept until his wife came with another glass of that unappetizing medicine. He drank it, kept awake until after supper, and slept like a stone until the following morning. When Toby brought breakfast, Lockwood sat up in bed. She examined his wounds, drew back, sat to watch him eat, and eventually said: "The inflammation is almost gone. How do you feel?"

Lockwood smiled at her. "Better'n I've felt since I rode away." His smile lingered. "In'ian medicine heap good."

She laughed. He hadn't heard that sound for a long time. He said: "Ma'am, if you was in the mood . . . !"

She sprang up, went as far as the door with the empty glass in her hand, looked at him, shook her head, and disappeared.

That evening, when Jim arrived, Lockwood was sitting up. His eyes were clear, and his color had improved. The younger man sat at bedside with his hat on the floor. Lockwood asked if he had learned anything. Jim brightened. "I roped a stump."

"First cast?"

"No, but I got it on the fourth one. I never used a lariat before. Tomorrow we're goin' farther out. Evan says it's not too early to begin the gather . . . drift 'em closer so's when it's time, we won't have to ride all over hell makin' a roundup."

When Francesca appeared in the doorway, Jim left. He was not comfortable around either of the women at the main house. In fact he was not comfortable around women anywhere.

Francesca made a slight sniffing sound after Jim had eased around her on his way out. "You are his friend?" she asked, and Lockwood nodded. "Then tell him to take a bath and to change his clothes. When I was small, my father's brother took me on a boar hunt. I was a good rider. Did you ever smell a boar pig?"

Lockwood shook his head.

"But you smelled *him,* so now you know. I came to ask if you would like to eat anything more before you go to sleep."

Lockwood was full from supper. "I'm fine, Francesca. No thanks, no more to eat."

She nodded from the doorway. "You look better."

"I feel better."

She was turning when she also said: "No one knows everything, do they? Even Indians we can learn from. Good night."

Chapter Twenty

THE SECRET

True to his word on the fifth day Doctor Smith returned. He had a new top buggy. It had yellow wheels, a black body, and red leather upholstery inside. The harness was also new; it was a California driving harness. There was no collar pad, collar, or hames.

Lockwood was sitting on the porch, wrapped in a blanket he did not need nor want but which his wife and Francesca insisted he use. He called to the physician. "Mighty pretty rig. The pill-rollin' business must be good."

The tall Indian smiled, came up onto the porch, sat down, and pushed his hat back. He was admiring his new buggy when he said: "White man, horse-pull buggy cost one hundred and fifty dollars."

Lockwood grinned. "Big rich In'ian peddle medicine."

They both laughed. The doctor faced Lockwood. "How do you feel?"

"I feel fine. I'm sort of weak gettin' around."

Smith nodded knowingly. "It takes time." He paused before also saying: "A man you are. You're in good shape. You'll be back in the saddle by trail time. Unless you get hurt again. By the way, Bertha an' the blacksmith sent their regards."

It was past noon, but Lockwood asked the physician if he'd like something to eat. Smith declined, shoved out his legs, relaxed in verandah shade, and gazed over the countryside. "I've heard a lot about you in town, Mister Lockwood. It started when you shot three freighters years back."

"Two, Doctor. Someone else shot the third one from a dog-trot."

Francesca appeared soundlessly with two glasses of lemonade. She nodded when they thanked her and disappeared back inside.

"How did the redskin medicine work?"

Lockwood considered the doctor when he said: "Like a charm. My wife 'n' I been wonderin' . . . ?"

"The Indians used it since long ago, Mister Lockwood. They'd take some plants they knew about, wet 'em, put 'em where they wouldn't get sunlight and, when they rotted, the Indians would scrape off the rot. That's what they cured infections with." Dr. Smith made a small, tired smile. "You know it works, an' I know it works. But you just try to tell a physician about using mold to cure infections and see how he'll look at you." Dr. Smith put the empty glass aside, shot to his feet, facing Lockwood. "Someday, maybe, but not now. Indians don't know anything."

Lockwood changed the subject. "How many horses do I owe you?"

Smith smiled. He had strong, white teeth. "I got a horse. I got to buy hay for it because I keep it in town. How about five dollars?"

Lockwood dove into a pocket, pulled out some worn greenbacks, peeled off several, and handed them to the Indian who counted them and raised his eyes. Lockwood winked. "The extra's so's you can make bottles of medicine for folks who wouldn't take it if they knew what it was. Doctor, come back any time."

They shook hands. The physician went down to untie his animal. He climbed into the buggy and waved as he drove out of the yard.

That night Lockwood told his wife about the medicine. She looked straight at him without speaking. Lockwood sighed to himself. Hell, even a person who had seen it work didn't believe it. Later, when they were in bed Toby said: "I didn't know they had a sense of humor."

"Who?"

"Indians."

Four days later Lockwood rode out with Evan, who told him the "lad," as he called Jim, had the makings of a top hand. "Takes to the work like a duck in water."

"Has he mentioned moving on?"

Evan looked surprised. "Not to me he ain't. Is that what he's goin' to do?"

"Not if I can help it, Evan."

Lockwood rode out every few days. He tired easily for a week or two, but that was temporary. His side was healing. There would always be an ugly scar. The arm was also badly scarred, but in time Lockwood could use it without pain. He was just not quite as good a roper as he had been, but he was still good enough.

They were heading into autumn. Leaves were turning color. The sky was a pale, cold, unblemished blue. Evenings chilled off quickly, but the days were perfect, warm without being hot, brisk, the kind of weather that put a kink in the backs of horses at first saddling.

Jim was as good a hand as the other hired riders. He would not be as good as Evan or Lockwood for a long time yet and, one early morning when the men were saddling to ride out with a rind of ice on the trough, something happened that would make it even longer before Jim could equal Evan or Lockwood.

It was, everyone agreed afterwards, his own fault. No horseman mounted inside a building, that was one of the first things fathers taught sons. Marshal Duffy had been similarly a fool, but Jim was not aware of that. One must always lead a horse out into the open before mounting. If a horse is going to break in two, he will do it as soon as whoever is leading him gets him untracked. Sometimes it is caused by an icy saddle blanket on a warm back. Other times it could be an ice-cold mouthpiece stinging a horse's tongue when he is bridled.

This time there was no reason, or there were several. The men who saw it happen never afterwards unanimously agreed about the cause. They were too surprised when Jim stepped into the stirrup and swung across the saddle without untracking the horse first.

They had no time to yell. The horse stuck his head between his shanks and bucked three times as hard as he could standing in one place. The third pitch sent Jim sailing. He fetched up against the bulk of the harness room so hard the onlookers could hear the wood crack.

He was knocked senseless. One man went after the horse, stripped it, and turned it into a corral out back. The others, including Evan Turlock, moved Jim so that he could lie flat out. One of them went to the house for Lockwood.

When he arrived, Evan stood up shaking his head. "He hit the side of the doorway so hard we could hear the wood crack. It knocked him cold."

Lockwood knelt to feel for broken bones. He probed very gently for what he dreaded — a cracked skull. There was none. Every bone was solid. He stood up. He leaned to lift the youth, but Evan shouldered him aside.

They carried him to the main house, put him in an unused bedroom where Toby and Francesca made their own examination. The riders departed. They had work to do. It was close to the time for rounding up all salable critters and start south to the railroad yards.

They put Jim under the covers after removing his boots. Lockwood waited until the youth groaned, opened his eyes, looked around, finally looked at Lockwood as he raspingly asked: "What happened?"

"You got bucked off," Lockwood told

him. "Jim, don't ever mount a horse inside a barn, or until you've turned him a time or two."

Toby looked disapprovingly at her husband. Right now the lad needed care not scolding. She said: "If you're going with the men, you'd better hurry."

They exchanged a look. Lockwood nodded and left. Francesca said: "There is blood beginning on his back."

Toby nodded. "Roll over, Jim."

He obeyed and groaned from the effort. There was indeed a thin streak on his back from the shoulders half way down, which had not been there before.

Francesca said: "I'll get some hot water and clean rags."

Toby nodded without speaking. She leaned to roll Jim onto his side so she could unbutton the shirt. She could not get it entirely off. She left his right arm in the shirt as she eased him back down on his stomach. This time he did not groan.

She stood still, looking at his back. He heard her go to a chair and sit down. He turned his head. She was sitting there, expressionless, staring at his back. He said: "Are you all right, ma'am?"

Toby didn't answer. She pushed up out of the chair and was waiting when Francesca arrived with the basin and clean rags. Without looking at either of them, Toby gently washed the streak of blood off, dried her hands, and turned without a word.

She went as far as the parlor where she stood in front of the window, looking down across the yard. Her husband was over at the shoeing shed selecting horseshoe blanks. He had the forge fired up with a large bay horse cross-tied. She watched him pump the forge, using long-handled tongs to set the shoes, three around the edge, one directly into the fire.

He occasionally gave the bellows a pump, went to the horse, lifted a forefoot, skived it lightly, got the hoof level, and turned back to take the cherry-red shoe from the forge and begin to shape it at the anvil. She had always liked the sound of steel being warped at an anvil.

When Lockwood had the shoe hammered level, he stuck a pointed steel pin into a nailhole, took the shoe to the horse, squinted when he touched the shoe to the hoof so rank smoke would not bother him, lifted the shoe away, studied where it had singed, dropped the foot, and dunked the shoe into the water barrel where steam arose.

She watched him fit and nail two shoes. As he was working up the last two, she shed her apron and walked slowly across to the shed. Lockwood looked up from his bent-over position where he was nailing, gazed at her for a moment, looked down, clinched the nails, four on each side, and dropped the hoof.

She was leaning in the opening. He sluiced off at the oak barrel, dried himself with a large blue bandanna, and approached her. A man couldn't live with a woman as long as Lockwood had lived with his wife and not understand their moods and expressions. But this time, while he understood the stricken look, he misinterpreted it. He thought she had come to tell him something was terribly wrong with the injured youth.

He said: "Toby . . . ?"

She returned his gaze without answering for a moment. "He is your son, isn't he?"

Lockwood used the blue bandanna again although his hands and arms were dry. "Yes."

She did not smile, but she spoke softly. "It's all right, Cuff. But when I saw his back. The same birthmark, only fainter. Is that why you rode away?"

"No. I didn't know who he was until his shirt got torn." He looked around for something to sit on, found an old rough-wood horseshoe keg, and eased down on it. She watched him. "Does he know?" she asked.

Lockwood shook his head.

"Hadn't you ought to tell him?"

He nodded, still silent as he regarded the dozing bay horse.

For a long time she leaned in the doorway, looking at him. Eventually she straightened up, stepped over, put a hand briefly on his shoulder as she said: "Cuff, you can't handle it."

He looked up quickly. "Yes, I can."

"Then why didn't you tell him on the trail?" She squeezed his shoulder, bent swiftly to kiss his cheek, and turned back toward the main house. He remained on the barrel watching, until she went up to the porch, opened the door, and closed it after herself.

He arose, moved heavily back to the forge, pumped it several times, then went back to work on the bay horse. He worked mechanically, doing things by instinct and experience. Shoeing a horse was pretty much repetition. After the first ten or fifteen everything just sort of fell into a sequence. Providing there were no pinched heels, scarred quarters, other abnormalities which required corrective shoeing, a man in his fifties who had shod horses off and on all his life could do a good job while his mind was thoroughly detached.

Lockwood shed the mule-skin apron, cleaned up at the trough, and led the bay horse across the yard, down through the barn, and turned him into a corral out back. He then went back, half way through the barn, got weak in the legs, and sat down on an old bench. He rolled and lighted a smoke, never once remembering a law of every ranch yard. Don't smoke in the barn.

He was still sitting there an hour later when he heard someone crossing from the main house. He looked up, expecting to see his wife.

Jim walked in out of the sunlight and stopped. Lockwood got up slowly. "You hadn't ought to be walkin'," he said.

The youth stood, looking straight at Lockwood. It was hard for him, too. He said: "Your wife told me."

Lockwood let his breath out slowly, and waited. There may have been a time for him to explain, maybe back on the trail. Now, since he hadn't told the lad, someone else had. He did not have the initiative. Jim had it.

They stood looking at each other for a long time until the younger man came closer, looking for something to sit on. His back ached.

Lockwood stepped clear of the horseshoe keg and nodded toward it. Jim went that far but did not sit. Instead he faced Lockwood. "You could have told me," he said.

Lockwood nodded dumbly. "Sit down. Take the weight off your back."

Jim remained standing. "Why didn't you?"

"I thought about it. On the ride back I didn't hardly think of anything else."

Jim sat down on the keg, watching Lockwood.

"I didn't know how you'd take it. I didn't know exactly how to tell you about your mother an' me. It just happened, Jim. There's no other way to explain it. It just happened. I didn't know she was dead. I had no idea there'd been a child." Lockwood paused. "I had a strong feelin' I should go back, so I went." Lockwood moved to lean against a stall door. He did not explain about the dream; in fact he never told his son about the dream. Jim sat slumped, gazing at the earthen floor of the barn.

Lockwood had little more to say. "It's up to you, son. Nothing I can tell you will make it seem right. Maybe it wasn't right. I sure believe now it wasn't. But back then . . . springtime, her sittin' there smilin'. It was a beautiful, blessed time. We shared it."

"And you rode on."

"Yes."

"Toby's a wise woman," Jim said, without looking at his father. "I never met anyone like her before."

Lockwood nodded about that. "Most likely you never will again, either."

Jim arose, grimaced for a second before facing Lockwood. "She said what's done is done. She said folks can't undo things no matter how much they want to. She said you didn't do nothin' wrong. You were a young buck back then. It was that time of year. Just answer one question for me. If you'd known there'd been a child, would you have come back?"

Lockwood had no difficulty answering. "I'd have come back from wherever I was."

Jim did not smile at his father, but he shoved out a callused hand. After they had shaken, each with a hard grip, Lockwood had a question of his own to ask. "Did you tell Evan an' the others your name was Jim Rider?"

"No. Just Jim. I wouldn't have told them the Rider part of it. I hate that."

"Would you mind tellin' them your name is Jim Lockwood?"

"No."

Jim might have said more but Francesca

rang the meal-time bell. They walked together to the house. Toby was standing in the middle of the parlor. As they shed their hats, Jim looked at his father. "I don't know what to call a step-mother."

His father answered shortly: "Ma'am," and looked at his wife.

She nodded.

Francesca, who knew every fact and every secret of the ranch, appeared in the kitchen doorway dry-eyed and flushed from standing over a hot stove. She said: "Jim, I told you not to leave that bed. After you eat, you get back in there."

He nodded, followed his father and stepmother into the kitchen, and did not surprise anyone when he ate like a horse. Francesca rolled her eyes.

When Lockwood and his wife were alone on the verandah with dusk coming down, he smiled at his wife. "Thank you, Toby."

"You're welcome, Cuff. I've been thinking about something I never told you. Do you remember when I said my husband and I were too busy to think about anything but the ranch?"

He remembered and nodded.

"Men are thick as oak. I knew when I said it you hadn't the faintest idea about what I meant."

He nodded about that too.

"I meant children." She paused, softly frowned, and also said: "But I didn't expect one to be eighteen years old when I got him."

They laughed, listened to a distant wolf howl, and held hands until night came, then went inside.

About the Author

Lauran Paine who, under his own name and various pseudonyms has written over 900 books, was born in Duluth, Minnesota, a descendant of the Revolutionary War patriot and author, Thomas Paine. His family moved to California when he was at an early age and his apprenticeship as a Western writer came about through the years he spent in the livestock trade, rodeos, and even motion pictures where he served as an extra because of his expert horsemanship in several films starring movie cowboy Johnny Mack Brown. In the late 1930s, Paine trapped wild horses in northern Arizona and even, for a time, worked as a professional farrier. Paine came to know the Old West through the eyes of many who had been born in the previous century and he learned that Western life had been very different from the way it was portrayed on the screen. He served in the U. S. Navy in the Second World War and began writing for Western pulp magazines following his discharge. It is interesting to note that all of his earliest novels (written under his own name and the pseudonym Mark Carrel) were published in the British market and he soon had as strong a following in that country as in the United States. Paine's Western fiction is characterized by strong plots, authenticity, an apparently effortless ability to construct situation and character, and a preference for building his stories upon a solid foundation of historical fact. ADOBE EMPIRE (1956), one of his best novels, is a fictionalized account of the last twenty years in the life of trader William Bent and, in an off-trail way, has a melancholy, bittersweet texture that is not easily forgotten. MOON PRAIRIE (1950), first published in the United States in 1994, is a memorable story set during the mountain-man period of the frontier. In later novels such as TEARS OF THE HEART (Five Star Westerns, 1995), he has showed that the special magic and power of his stories and characters have only matured along with his basic themes of changing times, changing attitudes, learning from experience, respecting nature, and the yearning for a simpler, more moderate way of life.